LOUISA JUNE
AND THE
NAZIS IN THE
WAVES

LOUISA JUNE
AND THE
NAZIS IN THE
WAVES

L. M. Elliott

KATHERINE TEGEN BOOKS
An Imprint of HarperCollins*Publishers*

Katherine Tegen Books is an imprint of HarperCollins Publishers.

Louisa June and the Nazis in the Waves
Copyright © 2022 by Laura Malone Elliott
All rights reserved. Printed in Lithuania.
No part of this book may be used or reproduced in any manner
whatsoever without written permission except in the case of
brief quotations embodied in critical articles and reviews. For
information address HarperCollins Children's Books, a division of
HarperCollins Publishers, 195 Broadway, New York, NY 10007.
www.harpercollinschildrens.com

Library of Congress Control Number: 2021945751
ISBN 978-0-06-305656-5

Typography by Carla Weise
21 22 23 24 25   SB   10 9 8 7 6 5 4 3 2 1
❖
First Edition

FOR MEGAN AND PETER—
MY WINDS, MY SAILS,
AND MY RUDDER.

I'm not afraid of storms,
for I'm learning how to sail my ship.

—LOUISA MAY ALCOTT, *LITTLE WOMEN*

NAZIS IN THE WAVES

Four days after Japan's surprise attack on Pearl Harbor in December of 1941, Germany also declared war on the United States. Its führer, Adolf Hitler, immediately unleashed a "wolfpack" of U-boat submarines to our East Coast. Their mission: to torpedo as many US cargo ships carrying fuel, military supplies, and food as possible. The submarines typically attacked in the dark of night, always without warning.

America was totally unprepared.

The first sinking: January 13, 1942, just three hundred miles off Cape Cod. An unseen torpedo launched by U-boat 123 cut an enormous freighter in half, killing eighty-seven sailors and passengers.

The next night, the same U-boat, U-123, tuned into New York City radio stations and followed the beam of Long Island's lighthouse at Montauk Point. The submarine's Nazi crew easily spotted its next victim, backlit and plainly silhouetted by the blaze of lights in homes and businesses along New York's coastline—the oil tanker Norness. *Three torpedoes took it down.*

U-123 continued on, following Long Island's shoreline. Within a few hours it attacked another oil carrier. This time just off the Hamptons. An enormous fireball flared six-hundred-and-fifty feet into the air, sending frightened residents of the exclusive beach communities scrambling in panic. The tanker sank in ten minutes.

Surfacing, U-123 cruised past Coney Island, past yachts moored for the night, right into New York City's Upper Bay. A photographer on board took snapshots of the Statue of Liberty and the illuminated Manhattan skyline, and German newspapers gleefully printed images they claimed came from the submarine.

Ten days later, almost four hundred miles to the south—where the Chesapeake Bay opens to the Atlantic Ocean at Norfolk, Virginia—another Nazi sub, U-66, torpedoed the tanker Empire Gem. *In the light thrown across the waves by that ship burning, the crew of U-66 spotted the distant silhouette of an ore carrier. Pretending to be the Diamond Shoal lighthouse, U-66 flashed a signal that lured the* Venore *toward it. The sub sank that vessel, too, with two torpedoes launched at short range.*

What German submariners scornfully called "the Great American Turkey Shoot" had begun.

By March 1942, Hitler's handful of subs were sinking on average a ship a day along the American coastline—killing sailors, sending crucial cargo to the ocean's bottom, and leaving miles of burning waves, slick with oil and debris. One of the Nazis' favorite hunting grounds: the waters just off Tidewater Virginia and the Chesapeake Bay.

LOUISA JUNE

My mama has the melancholy. Always has. But recently it's gone from her customary pinkish-gray—like a dawn mist in the marshes, still hopeful and able to clear into bright blue with the right sprinkle of sunshine—to thick, storm-surge purple-black. Like rolling waves burning.

My brother Butler would tell me the best way to weather it would be to steer straight in and hold tight to the rudder. But it's hard for a being to not get lost in that swell of inky agony. Mama's been that way ever since the war arrived on our Tide-water Virginia doorstep. Ever since Nazi U-boats started swarming the waters around the Chesa-peake Bay.

Before that, Mama used to smile pretty easy. Even laugh.

That's my daily goal now. To reel in a real smile from her, not just a nibble of one. To help her find her way to shore, up out of the storm waters of her heart. But it's proving about as hard as surviving a voyage up our Atlantic Coast without being hunted down by Hitler's submarines lurking in the waves.

One of the best lifelines for Mama, being such a book lover and all, is a good story. But it needs to be told well or she's disappointed, which makes things way worse. So I should start with how things were before—before the tides of trouble rose up in our lives. That way you—and I, for that matter—can find a truer course through the waves.

THE
BEFORE
OF IT

CHAPTER 1

One morning in late March, Mama and I were sitting in our kitchen, awash in daffodils we'd cut the day before—big golden trumpets, little starbursts of white and lemon stripes, and buttery blossoms with bright-orange faces. Buckets and buckets of them that she had hoped to take to the annual Virginia Daffodil Festival in Gloucester. But Hitler declaring war on America eight weeks earlier had canceled it. A wispy fog of disappointment was gathering on her.

"Tell me something nice, sugar," she said.

I was used to this morning recitation. Mama's been asking me that my whole life, like I'm her morning cup of coffee. If she asked with a small smile, I knew she just needed a sip of something, like catching a whiff of honeysuckle when you're dragging yourself home after a long day of crabbing. It'll pick you right up. A little joke might work—even if she'd heard it a hundred times already.

If there was no smile but she still turned to look at me, she needed a little stronger brew. Painting a scene of happiness—maybe about a mockingbird settling in for a good sing in the lilac below my bedroom window, or the baby cottontail I spotted under the boxwood, or some tidbit of town scandal I'd picked up at the general store would do.

If Mama didn't move—spoke so soft I had to lean in to hear her—and was staring out the window as if an army of ghosts drifted among the wild water lilies, I could pour her pot after pot of "somethings nice" and she wouldn't revive.

This morning, I had an easy fix. There was big joy due at dinnertime. My daddy and my two oldest brothers—Will and Joe—would all be on shore leave from their merchant ships for a few days. For the first time in months, all seven of us would be together: Mama, Daddy, Will and Joe, my next-in-line siblings Katie and Butler, and then me, the baby of us all, bringing up the rear—like a little dinghy tethered to the ship, Daddy teases me.

"It'll be good to see Will and Joe, won't it, Mama?"

She brightened instantly. Fluttering up out of her chair, Mama started opening all our white-washed cabinets, checking food supplies. "We must make them a beautiful dinner, Louisa. I worry my boys starve on those ships. How good could a meal cooked in a tiny galley kitchen on the high seas be?"

I got up to help before she remembered the worries of the previous days—the reports of several merchant vessels like the ones Will navigated going missing once they'd sailed out of the bay. The terrible anxiety that maybe they'd been hit by Hitler's U-boats, which watermen families were beginning to realize were skulking offshore, waiting, like sharks that sometimes eyeball swimmers at Virginia Beach. No matter how much the navy or newspapers downplayed their presence. "Should we make them deviled eggs? Joe loves them," I suggested.

"Perfect! Please go to the henhouse, honey, and gather every egg, no matter how much the ladies fuss at you."

"Yes, ma'am." Out I skipped, knowing she was on course for a good day.

That evening Mama giggled—sweet and soft—as Daddy tucked a canary-colored jonquil behind her ear. "You woulda been queen for sure, Ruthie," he said.

"Goodness, Russell, as if an old married woman would be chosen queen of a daffodil festival." She patted his chest. "But you are gallant to say so." Mama paused. "What I might have had a chance at was for one of these blooms to be chosen best of show. My bulbs absolutely rejoiced into life this year. Look." She held out her arms toward the rainbow of yellow hues stretching along the tiled counter, the long oak table, and the worn-wood floor. "Gorgeous, don't you think?"

Daddy grinned at her. "Yes indeed."

Mama's pale, heart-shaped face pinkened prettily. Even at forty-five, she could blush. "I meant the flowers, silly. I know it's selfish of me, given all that's going on, but it does seem harsh to cancel the Daffodil Festival altogether. I just . . . well . . . it doesn't seem like it would hurt to host a moment of thinking on daffodils and what's beautiful in life." She bit her lip in self-reprimand. "What really matters, of course, is not being able to ship the blooms up north to Philadelphia and New York for Easter, given the new restrictions. That's a hundred dollars we won't make this year. I'm so sorry for that. If we'd planted winter wheat instead . . ." Mama trailed off.

Life in Tidewater Virginia was hard, all about farming, fishing the rivers and marshes spilling into the Chesapeake Bay, or going to sea to crew freighters and tankers. On land, corn, beans, watermelons, and tomatoes did all right in our sandy soil—and daffodils. But you'd just barely get by with farming, given the Great Depression, plus the unknowns of drought or late frosts that could lay waste to crops. Most families—like mine—needed to do a combination of all three to keep our heads above water money-wise.

My family was luckier than most—Daddy was a tugboat captain, his employment steady, his white captain's cap marking him as special the moment he walked out of our house, heading to port in Norfolk. But that also meant most of the time he was off hauling barges, chugging along the Chesapeake or out into the Atlantic. That left Mama to run our seventy-acre farm and tend to our rowdy brood. She'd been the one to make the decision to till some of our fields in jonquils.

A lot of daddies wouldn't have been too happy about that. You can't eat daffodils.

"I'm afraid all the runs up the coast nowadays are going to concentrate on the war effort, moving oil, gasoline, and the makings of ammunition," Daddy answered Mama. "We've got a lot of catch-up to do to Hitler's forces—and pronto.

No more direct steamers for tourists or flowers to New York City. We'll just sell the daffodils in Richmond, sweetheart."

"We won't get the same amount as we would from city florists up north," Mama murmured as she waded through the golden bower past my brothers and sister to the kitchen sink and window. Suddenly fretful and second-guessing herself, she stood picking at her apron. She gazed out past the chicken coop, the hog pen, and the woodshed, down toward the Back River's northwest branch that lapped our wharf. "Such a waste," she sighed, a dragging anchor of regret in her voice.

Butler made it to her side before I could.

The sun was setting, spilling a red glow along the high-tide waters up to our acres that still danced with rows and rows of yellow buds about to open.

Closing his blue-gray eyes, Butler recited: "*Continuous as the stars that shine and twinkle on the milky way, they stretched in never-ending line, along the margin of a bay.*" He put his arm over her shoulders, protective. "Just like Wordsworth said, Mama. Your host of dancing daffodils outdo *the sparkling waves in glee*. I bet all the watermen passing by the farm feel their hearts leap up in happiness, for just a moment, thanks to you."

Awww, my two other brothers and my sister crooned.

"Amen, Brother," added Will, the oldest.

Mama melted. She hugged Butler tight, her smile returning. She'd named him for William *Butler* Yeats, her favorite poet when she'd been studying at Hollins College, hoping to become a writer or a fancy New York City editor, or a teacher maybe. According to family lore, Butler's birthing was hard and long, and Mama had asked my grandmother to read bits of Yeats's poems aloud to her to get her through the contractions.

I swear that sealed Butler's destiny. At seventeen years old, he was all lyrical sweetness, like early morning birdsong. And smart. Smarter than all of us put together. He'd just won a scholarship to William & Mary. Butler would be going off to Williamsburg come September. I was going to miss him something dreadful when he left.

I tried to find something equally literary to say. After all, Mama—seeing how near-perfect Butler turned out—decided to name me in homage to the author of *Little Women*. Too bad I was born in June, because that became my middle name. Had I timed things better, maybe I could have been Louisa May instead of Louisa June, and been better inspired.

Before I could think of anything, Will dove in and hoisted Butler without a grunt of effort even though Butler was six feet tall. Lean and willowy, like a sycamore sapling—but still, a considerable weight to just scoop up. Will paraded him around the kitchen as if Butler were a toddler, whooping and carrying on about his baby brother being a smarty-pants.

Joe fell in right behind Will. "College boy, college boy," he chanted.

Katie brought up the rear, plucking a few daffodils from the dozen buckets and tossing blossoms at Butler as if he were some anointed prince.

Daddy guffawed.

Mama beamed.

After three rotations around the daffodils, Will put Butler down. He and Joe slapped him on the back, while Katie tickled his stomach.

"Quit it, y'all." Butler swatted at them and squirmed away. "You could have gone to college too, you know."

"Me? Ha!" Will chuckled.

"Yeah, that dog don't hunt," Joe joked, needling Will good-naturedly.

"Say what?" Will pretend-punched Joe's stomach.

Joe fake-pummeled back.

Katie thwacked their heads with a daffodil.

The three of them finally stopped their ruckus, and Will, grinning, said, "We just ain't book learners like you, Butler. I prefer reading the tides and the winds."

Will was undercutting himself bad. At twenty-three years old, my oldest brother had already risen to the rank of Second Mate, in charge of navigating enormous ships through the shoals of the Chesapeake capes and then along the high seas to Boston or beyond. That took sizeable skill. You know how big those things are? A freighter carries cargo that's equivalent in bulk to four trains, each pulling seventy-five loaded cars!

"Besides," Will concluded, "when I was your age, baby brother, thirty-two dollars a month as an able seamen looked mighty good. Right, Daddy?"

Daddy nodded. "You're darn tootin', son." Then he grew thoughtful. "You really get to know the soul of a man, watching him ride out thirty-foot breakers while standing watch. That's a good book, too, I'd say."

Will elbowed Joe.

Just thirteen months younger than Will, Joe had also gone to sea straight out of high school. For the past three years, he'd been working Daddy's tug as his radioman. Clearly, Will expected Joe to say, "Aye, aye, Captain."

But Joe awkwardly stepped away from Will's ribbing. He pushed back a flop of honey-colored hair from his eyes and stuck his hands in the back pockets of his dungarees. Looking down, Joe started twitching his foot around, nervous-like, as if he were after a bug.

Daddy cocked his head. "Something on your mind, son?"

"Go on," Katie whispered. "Tell him." She and Joe shared secrets the way I'd always wished Katie and I did. My sister and I shared a bedroom, but I guess the five years' difference in our ages was too big a sea to whisper across. Although now that I was thirteen-going-on-fourteen I sure felt deserving of her confidences.

"Tell what?" Mama asked nervously.

All playfulness died. I could hear the ancient grandfather clock in the hallway tick.

"Everything's different now, Mama," said Joe hesitantly. "We're at war. And the Axis is serious about it. It only took—what? A month after Pearl Harbor—for Hitler's U-boat submarines to make it across the Atlantic to start taking down our cargo ships?"

"First attack was mid-January," Will chimed in, his mirth instantly gone. "The war department is censoring the news, but the scuttlebutt on the docks is that attacks are happening every night now. And that one torpedo can sink a tanker in ten minutes flat." Will broke off with a grimace. "God-awful way to go."

Daddy put his hand on Joe's shoulder. "So . . . what are you thinking, boy?"

"Well, sir . . ." Joe straightened up tall. Like Daddy and Will, he was taut and permanently sun-bleached, whittled by gales and hard work. That kind of young man stood naturally at attention. "Hitler's tinfish caught us with our pants down. Most of what's left of our navy after Pearl Harbor is in the Pacific. Here on the East Coast we've got bupkis—just that rust bucket, the *Dickerson,* patrolling all of Virginia and North Carolina's coastline. The game the Krauts are playing—trolling our waters looking to sink all the supplies we're trying to get to England, or to starve out our own American cities—well, geez—it could take us to our knees before we even get ourselves ready to fight.

"Sooo." Joe drew in a long breath before dropping his depth charge of news. "I've signed up for the navy, Daddy. I leave for Seabee training in Norfolk next week. Sorry to leave you shorthanded, but I know you can find another radio guy easy enough. The navy needs men who can man the wires. I'll help the country more on a destroyer." He pivoted slowly toward Mama, his freckled face hopeful. "Proud of me?"

All eyes turned to Mama. Her face furrowed.

"Mama?" Joe murmured.

Still she hesitated, mesmerized by something only she was looking at, like some ancient sooth-sayer of doom.

Joe started squirming.

I'd been the recipient of one of those far-off, anxious gazes of hers. It could run your blood cold imagining what she was seeing. So I grabbed the big-faced daffodils that had hit the floor as Katie flung them at Butler. Before Joe could realize what I was doing, I tiptoed to him and held up those daf-fodils behind his head—like bunny ears you make when clowning around during a photograph.

Mama burst out laughing.

Then Daddy, then Will, then Katie, then Butler.

"What the heck?" Joe whirled around. "Okay, Miss Jokester." He caught me up and swung me around the way he had when I was little.

By the time Joe put me back down Mama had recovered. She kissed Joe's cheek. "I'm always proud of you, sweetheart." Glancing around the room, she added, "Of all of you. Although you, Miss Louisa June," she tapped my nose, "still need a little work."

Will punched Joe's shoulder. "You son of a gun."

"Join with me."

Will shook his head. "If der führer keeps sinking our cargo ships at this rate the swastika will be flying over the White House before you know it. The US of A needs navigators like me staying in the merchant marine moving oil and ore and airplane parts and supplies. But . . . I'll feel a lot better when you're on a destroyer to my starboard as escort to my convoy"—he grinned, nabbing Joe into a headlock and ruffling his hair—"little brother."

CHAPTER 2

A few days later, I closed my book and ran my hand over its cover drawing of Mary Poppins with her parrot-head umbrella. Wouldn't it just be the best to be able to slide *up* a banister like she does? I'd read the book when I was younger, sure, but I kept rereading it because I was starting to catch some of the adult humor tucked into its lines. My cousin Belle—who owns most every good book there is, I think—told me that a story can speak to a soul different ways at different times, getting better with every reading.

I also loved the book's London scenes. The city sounds so beautiful and magical. I hope to see it with my very own eyes someday—if London survives Hitler's Luftwaffe dumping bombs on it night after night.

"What's a cockney?" I asked aloud.

We were in the middle of our nightly library hour—as Mama called it—after dinner, after listening to the radio, when we all settled into different chairs, haloed by lamplight, and dove into worlds conjured by words. When I asked my question, Mama just nestled deeper into her faded chintz armchair, barely reacting—like she'd been dangling her feet in the water and gotten tickled by a minnow passing by—she was that submerged in her book.

I repeated my question to Daddy.

Without looking up from his weekly mariner newspaper, *The Pilot*, he answered, "Someone from London's East End."

"Have you known any?"

"Yup. Used to sail with a bunch of them when I was still crossing the Atlantic on freights, before starting to tug. And a couple during my war." Daddy was referring to the time he served in the navy during what used to be called the Great War—the war to end all wars supposedly—and just recently been branded World War I by *Time* magazine. Daddy had gone straight from high school to crewing a merchant ship to support his widowed mother and siblings when his own father's boat was lost in a storm—like many Tidewater watermen do. So when the Germans, Brits, and French tried to annihilate each other that go-round, he was all prepped and ready to step in and help our navy.

Just like Joe was doing now, following in Daddy's wake, twenty-three years later.

"Really?" I asked.

Daddy nodded and turned a page. "That's the one thing I do miss about those transatlantic voyages—meeting 'blokes,'" he smiled, using an odd accent, "from all over the world."

"What's London like?" I asked, awed.

"You know, I never made it there. Was coming in and out of Liverpool." He snapped his paper to make the newsprint pages stand up straight. "Don't that beat all," he muttered.

"What, Daddy?"

He kept reading and then snort-laughed. "Ruthie, listen to this."

Mama didn't budge. Cousin Belle had just lent her a new book titled *Rebecca*, and clearly it was a page-turner.

"Go ahead, Daddy, I'm listening," I said.

Butler stirred in his chair. "Me too."

"There's a story in here about a dozen survivors of a Nazi sub attack. Their cargo ship was hit because they'd been dimwitted enough to answer what they thought was another American ship flashing 'P' at them—you know, 'show your lights.' Thinking they were about to run into the other ship in the dark, they did. It was the Jerries, of course. Boom! Down that boat went.

"The guys drifted in a lifeboat for ten days, surviving on a biscuit a day before the coast guard found them. Guess where they got the supplies? The U-boat actually surfaced and tossed the crackers down to them. That German submarine captain even asked how the Dodgers were doing. A Kraut baseball fan! He'd spent his childhood in Brooklyn with his parents before returning to Germany. Right before that Nazi closed the hatch to order his crew to submerge and go after more Americans, he shouted, 'Give my best to President Roosevelt! I met him when I was a little boy.'" Daddy shook his head and folded his paper. "The world's gone all catawampus, that's for sure. But maybe some of these Germans aren't demons."

It was then Daddy noticed what my brother was reading—*Mutiny on the Bounty.* "Good grief, son! Isn't that a story about sailors setting their captain adrift in a rowboat on the high seas? Maybe it's a good thing you're not a member of my crew!"

The sound of a pickup truck making its way along our lane saved Butler from Daddy's teasing. A door slammed, and we could hear Katie calling, "Night! See y'all tomorrow."

At that, Mama looked up. Carefully marking her place with the little wooden swan bookmark Butler had whittled for her, she murmured,

"Katherine's home early. I hope everything is all right."

Sweeping into the parlor, my big sister flung the needlepointed clutch Mama had lent her onto the piano stool, before flopping into an armchair. She hoisted her legs over its frayed arm and swung them furiously.

Daddy laughed good-naturedly at her drama. "Something wrong, Katydid?"

"I should say so!" She flipped her chestnut curls off her shoulder. (How I wish I'd also gotten Mama's thick, glossy, wavy hair. Mine is like Daddy's, dishwater blond and straight. No matter how Katie has fussed over it with a curling iron trying to help me out with big-sister pity, it falls back to being a dull sheet of hay.)

Katie yanked off a pin she'd been awarded by the Red Cross for her regular attendance at its dances for trainees. Boys were being brought in to the Tidewater by the thousands, arriving by train at the dozen-plus military posts around Richmond, Norfolk, and Newport News. No one knew when the new soldiers and airmen would be ready to ship out through Hampton Roads to begin the fight against Hitler. In the meantime, the army needed to keep them occupied during off-duty hours. Carefully monitored dances with big bands and local girls seemed the solution on the weekends.

Katie took a deep breath, let it out in a long, long sigh, and said, "I was asked to leave the dance."

Everyone sat up.

"Whatever for?" asked Mama.

"I got into an argument with a recruit who was getting a little too friendly with Emma."

"They . . . they asked you to leave? Not the soldier?" Mama was appalled.

Katie smirked, rolled her eyes, and gave Mama a look to say: Isn't that the way of things?

Daddy was furious. "They booted my little girl because of some pushy, hot-to-trot jackass?" He stood. "What's the name of the stuck-up grand dame who did that, Katydid? I'm going to give her what for."

Katie grinned, clearly gratified by Daddy's

outrage. "I believe they asked me to leave because," she paused, trying unsuccessfully to mask her amusement, "I might have . . . maybe . . . kicked him in the shins." She shrugged, holding up her hands in mock apology. "And golly, I feel ever so bad. The poor boy seemed to limp a little afterward."

Daddy doubled over laughing.

"That soldier should count his lucky stars that he survived the fray," Butler joked. "I've been on the other end of an argument with my big sis, and it isn't a safe place."

Katie smiled and blew him a kiss.

"Well, I don't think Katie should go back to those dances if the matrons aren't controlling the situation better, do you, Russell?" Mama said.

"Oh, Mama, I'm not going back." Katie turned serious. "Emma neither. I didn't know it, but they've actually been keeping records on us—the girls. *Our* behavior."

"I'm sure there's a string of gold stars by your name," Butler said. "Just like you always had at school."

She smiled fondly at him. "You always think the best of everyone, Butty. Nope. Just the opposite. Evidently I already had several marks against me—for refusing to dance with some guys and similar"—she paused to make quotation marks in the air—"'infractions.' Mrs. Dawson said . . ." Katie drew herself up and adopted the most ridiculous, self-impressed, high-society Virginia drawl. "'We've all had an eye on you, Miss Brookes, for quite a while. Yes, quite a while, I say. ALL of us.'"

"What?" Mama whispered at the same time Daddy bellowed, "WHAT?"

Katie kept reciting. "'We've tried to excuse your behavior out of respect for your lovely mother and her family. But we have made note, yes, indeed we have, made note I say, many of them in fact, about your less than agreeable behavior.'"

Mama turned red. "That's outrageous!"

I saw Katie hesitate just the littlest bit and smile to herself before she said the next thing. I'd seen that look before. Katie wanted something from Mama, and she'd used Mrs. Dawson's patronizing speech to prime the pump. "So, Mama, as you can see, I can't possibly go back to a place where I'm so . . . so," she put her hand atop her heart, "so . . . dishonored . . . so . . . so reviled." She paused with a pretty pout of indignation.

What was she up to, I wondered.

It only took about ten seconds to find out.

"And," Katie drew out the word, "I wouldn't want to anyway. I want to do more than just dancing with boys to keep them out of trouble on a Saturday." She paused again to make sure Mama and Daddy were listening carefully and then blurted out, "The Virginia Mechanics Institute is going to let girls take welding courses, starting next week."

Mama's mouth popped open.

Katie talked fast now, her words tumbling along like rapids. "Given those Nazis out there in the waves—watching, waiting, gunning for our boys—we need replacement boats built fast. The Newport News Shipbuilding Company is going to start spitting out a new ship design called the Liberty Boat. They can be welded together—not riveted—which means they can build a ship in a week as long as the company runs twenty-four hours in shifts. Because most men are going to be in the fighting forces, they'll be hiring women." She got out of her chair and knelt beside Mama's. "Please say yes."

"But . . . but . . ." Mama was flummoxed.

Daddy took up the slack. "There's talk of rationing gas soon, Katie. We won't have enough for you to drive our pickup there and back every day."

Katie had her answer for that ready. "Why, that won't matter a bit, Daddy. Emma and her sister have already rented a room in Newport News. A really nice widow they know is turning her big old brick home into a boarding house for girls. I can share the room with them. Emma's mama and daddy have given her permission. And you've always trusted their opinion. I'll catch the trolley that stops just a block away and then ride it straight to the dry docks. All safe and sound. Emma and I will keep watch over each other."

She put her hand on Mama's knee and lowered her voice. "Please, Mama. It'll be like the Barbizon Hotel in New York City that you've always told me you wanted to go live in and work at a publishing house. You know, back before Daddy. I can't just sit by, Mama, on backwaters during this fight—as much as I love home. I want to make a difference. You . . . you would, too, if you were me."

Mama reached out and stroked Katie's hair, thinking.

Daddy cleared his throat. I don't think he liked hearing about the Barbizon. "That'll leave your mama shorthanded when I'm on a run, Katydid," he said quietly.

I wasn't liking this conversation at all. I could see all manner of storm clouds drifting onto Mama's face. But this time I was more concerned with the ripples of this situation on me. The three of us—Katie, Butler, and I had been like the *Susan Constant, Godspeed,* and *Discovery,* the three little ships that brought the first settlers to Jamestown. We'd always sailed together. Plus, Katie and I had shared a bed and room all my life. Didn't she need to ask me about leaving, too? Especially with Butler going off to college in the fall. Was everything about our family going to change?

I glanced at Butler. He was frowning slightly, too.

I looked back at Katie. Her lively, freckled face was flushed with frustration. She caught my eye— the plea in hers clear.

Oh, all right, I thought. Just because I was the littlest didn't mean I couldn't do my part to help my siblings do theirs. Maybe if I did, everyone would stop thinking of me as a baby. Picking up Katie's chores might also mean I'd get some of the family's water duties instead of always being land-locked, gathering eggs and throwing slop at the hogs. That would mean more time with Butler this spring and summer, out around the oyster reefs, like I'd always craved. "I can take over Katie's chores," I announced.

Katie's return smile was pure sunshine.

For once Butler followed in my wake rather than the other way round. "She can be my first mate," he joined in. "Louisa's right handy with the sail, Daddy." He winked at me before continuing. "When she follows instructions."

"And I'll try to come home on the weekends to help, Daddy," Katie added.

Butler stood and tugged gently on my ponytail. "Wait until you take the rudder out there on the waters, little sis. You'll feel such . . ." He paused, reflecting. "Such freedom. There are such worlds out there." He closed his eyes—the telltale sign of his gathering his thoughts like a preacherman trying to find the spirit. After a moment he murmured, "Walt Whitman talks about . . . oh . . . hmm . . . the *different colors, pale gray and green, purple, white, and gold, the play of light through the water.*"

We all hushed for a moment, absorbing his poetic sermonizing. Butler's recitations elevated our daily life from grunt work and wearily counting the catch in a bushel basket, calculating its price, to a moment of beauty that made my heart skip a bit, like a stone thrown over still water.

"Okay, okay." Daddy held up his hands in surrender. "Your mama and I can't fight all three of you, can we, Ruthie?" But he ended by pointing his finger at Butler and me, adding, "Just make sure you bring back some oysters while you spout verse, all right?"

"Yes, sir!" Butler and I said together.

I could hardly wait.

CHAPTER 3

The next week, after Katie left with Emma and her sister for Newport News, I sat shivering slightly on our deadrise boat as Butler plunged sixteen-foot-long tongs into the water. We'd anchored in blue-green shallows adjacent to marshes just where the Back River met the open bay—right where he knew oysters clung together against the tidal waves in reefs along the bottom. The wind tugged at my coat and hair.

It was almost April, the sun bright, so the breezes were just warm enough to carry the slight tinge of salt sweeping inland from where the bay spread wide, opening its arms to embrace the Atlantic Ocean. But it was also laced with the perfume of plants daring to wake up and bud in the freshwater wetlands on shore. It wouldn't be until early May that the wild water lilies or irises would tentatively open their blossoms—one petal folding back at a time. But the chest-high cattails wading into the waters near us were definitely beginning to turn, green wicking up from their roots to flush new life into their winter brown. I sucked in the smells with joy, knowing spring would soon be coming in strong.

Butler shuffled carefully along the boat's flat-lipped edge, his red rubber boots squeaking. He grinned when he felt his submerged rakes scrape against a thick cluster of shells below. "There they are!" He worked the two long poles open-shut, open-shut, open-shut, to clamp onto and break the oysters' embrace, prying off the top tier. Then, grunting a bit with the effort, he lifted them, heavy with water, eelgrass, and dislodged oysters.

"Here's your first batch," he announced, dumping the shells onto the long, narrow culling table we'd laid like a tray across the width of the boat.

The oysters bounced and rolled before settling into a mucky brown heap. I wrinkled my nose. It must be said that the first human person to look at a crinkly oyster shell, covered with barnacles, mud worms, and sea squirts and decide that inside was a tasty treat had to have had a right big imagination. Or a terrible hunger.

Of course, the Powhatan tribes who lived here long before Jamestown's settlers arrived had basically lived off them. Their Algonquin word *Chesepiooc* meant "the great shellfish bay." Cousin Belle read me that out of one of her massive natural history books—she was a powerful good source for facts.

"Remember," Butler said, "throw back any that are smaller than three inches. They'll attach right back to the reef and grow bigger for us to catch next year. I always hate to disturb the colony like this— they create such castles of life down below. The old cradle the young so they can grow, oyster upon oyster, year after year. Minnows, grass shrimp, and crabs slip in and out of their protective nooks and crannies. A true peaceable kingdom."

I frowned looking at the oysters, plucked from such communion and lying in front of me. Now I was going to have a hard time swallowing them, just like I did whenever Mama decided to bake one of our hens for Sunday dinner.

"When it's warmer, the waters still and clear during low tide, we'll take a little swim so you can see the reef. Katie and I used to do it all the time. You need to hold my hand, though, as we dive. No being stubborn and pulling away, you hear?"

I nodded enthusiastically. The idea of diving in a cove with Butler made me as happy as . . . as . . . well, as a clam. Pulling my rubber gloves up over my elbows with a snap, I set to measuring. I threw the too-small oysters overboard. Then I knocked off spat—the pebble-sized babies who'd attached themselves onto grown-ups—from the ones big enough for us to keep. I threw the babies back in, too, like throwing a handful of coarse salt, and watched them sink to the colony below.

Butler observed me for a moment, saying, "Well done, matey." He dunked his tongs again.

Only about half of his first scoop of oysters ended up big enough to keep. I pushed those into a bushel basket, creating a thin layer, and waited for Butler to dump another jumbled mound in front of me. It'd take at least an hour of his plunging and raking and me culling to fill that basket. I hadn't really known how hard the work was before. No wonder everyone was snoring at bedtime so early in my house.

On the fourth or fifth time he raised those rakes and dropped a catch on the table with a loud clatter, Butler paused to rub his shoulders, sighing. "She's not going to be able to do this," he muttered. He was talking to himself, but I heard.

"Can too," I protested, standing up way too abruptly and setting the boat rocking. Thank goodness Butler had the balance of a cat, or he'd have gone into the water because of me.

But instead of being all irritated—I know I would have been at such landlubber carelessness—Butler laughed. "Louisa June, these things are heavy. When the tongs are full, I'm dredging up about twenty pounds of oysters. Hauling that up outta moving water is tough."

I bellied my way over to him, listing the boat. "Can too," I repeated, holding my hands up. "Let me try!"

"Girl, step back before you capsize us. If you really want to try, we'll do that next time. I'll show you how to work the poles off our wharf first. So you don't overturn us as you get the feel of them."

"Oh, all right," I grumbled.

Cocking his head, Butler said, "I love your spirit, Louisa, but don't forget to arm it with a little common sense, or you'll swamp yourself in trouble." He considered me a moment. "I . . . I hadn't counted on Katie being gone . . . when . . ." He paused.

When he left us for college and the outside world, I wanted to say. But I kept that bittersweet thought to myself for the moment because I could tell there was more coming from Butler, and I hung on every one of his words.

"Katie told me she'll be sending some of her pay home, but it won't be much, and she's got her own rent to worry over. I'll feel awful if my being gone means the family falls short of cash. . . . Maybe Emmett could help you with the fishing come fall?"

Emmett was the closest I had to a friend my own age. He and his family lived on the edge of our far acres. Oftentimes they helped pick our orchards and crops in exchange for keeping some of the fruit and vegetables for their own table.

"Could do, I expect." I couldn't help frowning a bit. I was still trying to adjust to the idea of Butler leaving and not complain about it. He was so excited. If I groused, it would be like a stray dog relieving himself all over our daffodils.

"Oh, listen!" he whispered, holding his hand up for silence. We both froze, hearing a great splashing and a high-pitched whooping. *Whoo-hoo, whoo-hoo.* Tundra swans—running along the water and flapping their enormous wings to lift up into the air. We turned in time to see a dozen angel-sized birds vault up from waters around a bend in the marsh grasses. Their wide, pearly wings swept in strong, urgent strokes as they climbed. When they passed over us, we could hear that magical, rhythmical *swish-swish-swish* as their feathers brushed air in perfect synchronicity with one another.

In an echo of splashes, another bevy scurried across the water's surface, flapping and whooping to launch themselves. The two flocks circled one another, quickly and easily gathering into an enormous V. Then, cued by the gorgeous swirl and *whoo-hoo*ing over our heads, another band of swans joined from farther south. The V reformed into an even bigger arrow of white slicing the blue heavens.

Shading our eyes against the sun, we watched the swans decide who was to be their point. Then they turned left, heading north. Leaving us for the wilds of northern Canada to nest and raise this year's young.

"Goodbye, beauties," Butler called. "See you

next winter." Then, after a moment, still gazing at the horizon, he recited:

> *All suddenly mount*
> *And scatter wheeling in great broken rings*
> *Upon their clamorous wings. . . .*
> *And now my heart is sore.*
> *All's changed. . . .*

He trailed off. I recognized the verse. It was a poem by William Butler Yeats, in fact—one that Mama read to us when the swans arrived for winter and searched our fields for scraps left on the ground during harvest. Butler stopped at the sad part, his face bathed in Mama-like melancholy—something I rarely saw on him. It made me feel squirmy, so I rushed in to add the poem's final lines:

> *Mysterious, beautiful;*
> *Among what rushes will they build,*
> *By what lake's edge or pool*
> *Delight men's eyes.*

I smiled proudly. "I wonder what their world is like up there near the Arctic? Don't you?"

Startled out of his revelry, Butler shifted his eyes down to me. "You know . . . you have the makings of a writer in you, Louisa. The way you watch things so carefully. The way you feel people's moods." He paused. "You be sure and make free use of my books while I'm at William & Mary." His characteristic dreamy look came back to his sweet face, thinking on college. "Don't forget, you hear?"

I nodded. "I won't." I didn't share that I'd already planned on raiding his personal library. A lump of bittersweet sadness choked my throat a bit, which was annoying, so I asked, "What's your favorite book?" I'd start by reading that one.

"Oh, golly, that's hard to pick. Maybe—" Butler broke off, looking over my head, beyond me. "What's that?"

Something bobbed in the slow waves, drifting toward us on the currents sweeping in from the ocean. Something dingy and mustard yellow, slightly submerged.

"Could it be a dead sturgeon?" I asked.

Butler shook his head, his expression alarmed.

It was an empty life jacket.

We agreed to not tell Mama about it when we got home.

"It probably fell off a boat belonging to some good-timing yachtsman, out for a Sunday sail and not paying any attention," Butler reassured me as he hauled it in and dropped in on our deck.

But I didn't believe him. The life preserver lay there, draining, beside our bushel of oysters, looking all beaten up and charred.

We'd heard tale of all sorts of debris floating in the tidewaters and up onto shore from boats hit by the Nazi U-boats just beyond the bay's opening. Bits of oars, planks, cans . . . and worse. Newspapers and the military remained mum. But alarmed whispers in church pews and the general store passed word of dead mariners being found and retrieved by fishermen. There was also a rumor that another tanker had just been torpedoed south of the bay, on its way toward North Carolina's

Outer Banks. Could a life preserver have floated all this way along the tides?

Neither of us spoke during the sail back to our farm's dock.

After we tied up, Butler took the preserver into the barn, asking me to wait with the oysters. Then together, he holding one handle of the basket and I the other, we staggered into the house hauling fifty pounds of shellfish between us.

"Oh my!" Mama gasped. "You must have five or six dozen oysters in there."

"Eighty-one," I answered.

"She's a natural oysterman," Butler pronounced as we lifted the shellfish and poured them into the thick cast-iron sink by the back porch door.

"Ooh . . . what a lovely oyster fry we can have before your Daddy goes on his run tomorrow," Mama said. Humming, she poured whipped eggs into a pie dish and cornmeal in another, the dipping and dusting for each oyster she'd drop into a sizzling skillet. Cornbread was already baking, filling the kitchen with its molasses-laced aroma, when Daddy entered.

He let the screen door slam shut behind him as he sniffed in appreciation. "Mm-hmm. Nothing better than coming home to a happy family and something delicious cooking in the kitchen. Are you about to make your county-famous fried oysters, Mrs. Brookes?" He hugged her and winked at me. "Looking at that pile of oysters in the sink, I can see you were a good hand today, Miss Lou."

"Yes, sir," I answered.

Butler came in behind Daddy. He'd been out throwing feed to our mules.

"Son," Daddy called out, all hale and hearty. "I have an opportunity for you."

"Yes, sir?"

"One of my crew is sick. And I'm already dealing with a green radio operator now that Joe is off with the navy recruits. How about you fill in? You'll make four dollars a day. Save up for your books this fall."

Mama's face turned gray. "Russell," she whispered, shaking her head vehemently.

"Oh, don't worry, sweetheart." He kept his voice breezy. "Nothing's happening to tugboats.

There are twenty or thirty of us working the coast every day—without a scratch. We're not worth firing a torpedo at. The Krauts are going after whales—tankers and big freighters—not minnows like us tugs. I'll just be pushing some barges of lumber to Philadelphia. And we'll only be gone four days, there and back."

"But what about his classes?" Mama protested.

"He's already accepted into college, Ruthie, nobody at the high school will care. And he'll be back in his desk before the end of the week."

"Four days. That's sixteen whole dollars," Butler murmured.

"Honey, you don't need that money," Mama said. "Your scholarship—"

"Pays for my tuition and a dorm room. That's all, Mama."

Daddy clapped him on the back. "Then this will be a fine start to saving up for food and books! Maybe you should crew with me over the summer—make a boatload of bucks. Well, a bucket anyway."

Mama stiffened and looked at Daddy with anxiety and frustration, but he kept chitchatting. He's like that—like a big ole overgrown hound puppy that can't help jumping all over you and slurping your face. "Aaaand," he drew out the word, "some pocket change for dates with a pretty coed."

Butler turned sunset red. "I don't know about dates, Daddy. I'll need to study hard to keep up."

"No, you won't," Mama said quietly. "You are the personification of the hunger to learn, sugar." She slipped her arm through his. "Everything soaks right in, straight to your heart, like a daffodil absorbing the sun." She rested her head on Butler's shoulder.

Daddy started rubbing his hands together. "Let's get to shucking, son. I can't wait to eat your catch. Come on."

Butler pulled away and Mama sighed, deflated, like a sail missing wind.

"I'll help you cook, Mama," I offered, taking her hand and squeezing. She forced a smile at me as Daddy and Butler took to prying open the shells with sharp knives—Daddy's blade quick and expert, Butler's methodical and reverential.

After a few minutes, Daddy sang out, "Well, would you look at that!" He was inspecting something in the oyster Butler had just forced open.

Butler turned, grinning. "I have a present for you, Mama." He held his hand outstretched. In his palm was a pearl.

When a Chesapeake oyster coughs up a pearl, it's usually small and gray. This one was the size of a pea and a gorgeous creamy green color—like a cloud-covered emerald.

"Now, that's a good omen if I ever saw one," Butler whispered as he pressed it into Mama's hand and kissed her cheek.

CHAPTER 4

The next evening, Mama and I puttered around a kitchen that felt awful empty. She'd grown quieter and quieter as the afternoon passed and twilight fell. "They left around six a.m., so averaging about five or six miles per hour they should be getting near . . . near Tangier Island by now," she murmured as she cracked eggs I'd brought in, still warm from the hens sitting on them. She beat them, distracted.

I waited.

She kept beating. A whole minute at least, maybe two.

"Mama?"

"Mm-hmm?"

"Want me to slice up the mushrooms?" Earlier in the day, she'd sent me into the woods to harvest some of the oyster mushrooms growing in shelves along the trunks of pine trees. She planned to make us a fine omelet, tasting woodsy and sweet. Nobody else I knew had omelets for dinner. She'd been inspired by some novel set in France.

"Yes, please," she answered, nodding.

I sliced.

She kept beating the golden pool in the bowl.

I finished cutting. She was still stirring, not noticing that the butter in the pan was starting to smoke. "Mama?"

"Mm-hmm?"

"Think the fry pan is hot enough now?"

"Oh, for goodness' sake," she reprimanded herself, pulling the pan off the flame for a moment to calm its surface heat down before pouring the eggs in, letting them spread out into a wide circle.

She gazed out the window as the eggs bubbled. I knew she was checking the skies. Thankfully, they were cloudless and peaceful. The Milky Way would be a beautiful thick swath of stars later, a dazzling sight out on the water. Butler would like that—a real gift for his first voyage.

"Mama?"

"Mm-hmm?"

"Want me to throw in the mushrooms?"

She didn't answer, frozen in that stare.

I threw them in, scattering them, accidentally-on-purpose knocking her elbow so she'd look down. Prompted, she folded the omelet overtop itself, its top nicely brown already.

Again the pan began to smoke. "Mama?"

"Mm-hmm?"

"Think it's ready."

Shaking her head slightly as if waking up, she cut the omelet in half with a wooden spoon and slid the wedges onto our plates. I carried them to the table and plunked myself onto the white-washed bench.

"Bless this food to our use and us to thy loving

service. Amen," I prayed without asking if I should. Hungry, I dug into her French-inspired meal.

She picked at hers.

I finished.

She'd only taken two bites.

Nibbling on a warm, buttered biscuit, I watched her break off a forkful of fluffy omelet. She lifted but dropped it back down on her plate before it reached her lips. Raising the fork again, she let out a gentle sigh and put it in her mouth.

I waited for her to chew, fighting off a sigh myself. This had the makings of a being a long, long night. Even though I was feeling the absence of Katie and Butler like a draft of cold air, I'd also actually been looking forward to having Mama to myself for a few nights for the very first time. I don't know what it was I'd been hoping we'd discuss, what motherly wisdom or tales from her early life. But an ill-at-ease, preoccupied silence hadn't been on my wish list.

The hall clock struck seven. The chimes reminded me that First Lady Eleanor Roosevelt was supposed to be broadcasting one of her evening chats right then. Thank the Lord! Something nice. Mama loved the first lady.

I popped up and snapped on our Zenith console radio. Out boomed an announcer's voice: *"Good evening. This is Mrs. Roosevelt's regular Sunday evening broadcast, sponsored by the Pan-American Coffee Bureau, representing eight good neighbor coffee-growing nations. This evening, Mrs. Roosevelt speaks to you from New York and gives you her impressions of the America of today: alert, hardworking, striving toward victory. But first, a few words from our sponsor . . ."*

Mama perked right up. "I totally forgot Mrs. Roosevelt is talking tonight. Turn it up a mite, would you, please?" She quickly finished her omelet and pushed away her plate to fold her hands together, completely attentive. I could see the student still in her.

The announcer shared a story from "somewhere in Africa" where RAF flyers were being treated to coffee sent from America: *"Think of the extra energy, the extra-steady nerves this coffee treat gave them. . . . Yes, and think what coffee can do for you, too, in these hectic, nerve-ruffling times. . . . And now, we present Mrs. Franklin D. Roosevelt."*

Mama squirmed in her seat to sit up straight and then bowed her head slightly to listen.

"Good evening, ladies and gentlemen. I'm sure that many of you who are listening to me tonight have had an opportunity to travel back and forth across our continent since December 7th. But for those who haven't . . . I should like to record my own impressions.

"People have taken first aid courses in great numbers, station wagons are in readiness for conversion into ambulances, and people know what their job is in case of need. There was an increased realization of . . . being wary of what you said and to whom you said it."

Mrs. Roosevelt went on in that slightly odd, high-pitched lilt of hers, talking about what ordinary citizens could do as the country scrambled to arm itself and to train brand-new G.I. Joe warriors. Especially mothers. *"I'm going to read ten rules which Mrs. Mabel Stillman of New York*

City has written for mothers in wartime, because they're sane and helpful, and everyone can follow them."

Mama stood and rushed to a drawer to pull out a note pad and pencil. She leaned against the counter and scribbled as Mrs. Roosevelt began. *"Rule 1: Before you turn on the news or open the mail, turn your hearts to God."*

"Rule 2: Keep breakfast cheerful and allow no controversy or personal criticism at any meal. May I interject that if your family is large and you can carry out Rule 2, you will start your day with a sense of accomplishment. I know of no meal where some members of the family are more apt to be slightly out of sorts."

Mama laughed. "How true! Mrs. Roosevelt is the mother of four boys and a daughter. Imagine raising that many children as well as helping her husband lead our nation during the horrors of the Depression and now this . . . this war. And to do all the charitable work she does." Mama had whispered all that as Mrs. Roosevelt could be heard shuffling her papers and clearing her throat.

"Rule 3: Buy wisely: practical clothing, healthy and simple food. Rule 4: Remember that working for your home and family is working for your nation. Rule 5: Stop parties but increase simple hospitality, especially to servicemen and their families."

Mama scratched furiously to keep up.

"Rule 6: Walk in the fresh air a few minutes every day. Rule 7: Look at beauty every day, if only the bare branches of a tree beside the park. Rule 8: Hear good music every day, if only a lullaby on the radio."

Mama nodded.

"Rule 9: Relax before the family comes home, and be ready to meet their problems. As a mother, a few years back, of an active family, this ninth rule I believe is one of the very best if you can possibly follow it . . . forget your own troubles as you take on those of others. Rule 10: Before turning out your light, lift your loved ones near and far, your country, and the whole world to the divine mercy, and end your day saying, 'Into thine hands I commit my spirit.' Perhaps if we can remember Rule

10, *we will ward off sleepless nights, for willy-nilly anxieties will lie heavily on many hearts, and there is nothing we can do about it.*"

Mama's pencil slowed during those last rules. She bit her lip as Mrs. Roosevelt concluded, *"Keep that quiet mind which is so essential."*

Mrs. Roosevelt went on to talk about victory gardens and the need to save jars for preserving, since a shortage of rubber rings was sure to come as the nation built a record number of military vehicles needing tires.

The male announcer took over. *"Thank you, Mrs. Roosevelt. As you have so well said, there is a new state of mind in this country, a true realization that each one of us must get the very most out of every minute of his or her working day. That's why more and more people, we are sure, turn to coffee, because they know that coffee does help give them extra energy and extra-steady nerves."*

Mama clicked off the radio and opened a cabinet to inspect her store of jars. The shelves were crammed full. "Good. We should be fine."

She closed the door and stood facing it for a

moment, and I could see her draw herself up taller. "A quiet mind," she repeated Mrs. Roosevelt's words. "Willy-nilly anxieties lie heavily on hearts. Yes. That Mrs. Roosevelt is a marvel." Squaring her shoulders, Mama turned toward me with a stunningly bright, reporting-for-duty smile. "We have our marching orders, don't we, sugar?" she chirped.

"Yes, ma'am!"

"Let's clean up now and have our library hour. I just finished *Rebecca*. What are you reading? If you're not in the middle of something, maybe we could read something aloud together?"

I'd just borrowed and started Butler's *Mutiny on the Bounty*. But I fibbed—saying I actually was in need of a new story. The chance to sit next to Mama and listen to her read? To be in her brain when it was happy? That was the exact kind of hope I'd had for this evening.

Mama looked immensely pleased. "What shall we read then?"

"What was your favorite book when you were my age?"

Mama didn't hesitate with her answer. *"Pride and Prejudice.* The protagonist—Lizzy—is deliciously funny. Knowing, independent—even when she falls in love." Mama paused, giving a little shrug. "In spite of herself." She playfully pinched my cheek. "She's very headstrong. Right up your alley, June-Bug."

Mama only called me that nickname when she was in high spirits. Mrs. Roosevelt just had that much of a positive impact on her. I helped Mama wash those dishes lickety-split before her mood could ebb.

CHAPTER 5

Twenty minutes later, Mama opened the Jane Austen novel—its leather-bound cover worn from a thousand readings—and I leaned up against her, tucking my feet underneath my butt on the living room's loveseat. She put her arm around me and drew me in closer, telling me to turn the pages for her. Awash in the light of that old lamp, on the chintz slipcovers' field of fabric peonies, feeling Mama breathing steady and peaceful, happiness settled in on me.

These were the moments we all lived for with Mama. When she was clear of those fogs of worry. When she smiled and looked us in the eye, and was right there, delighting in us, her most poetic, her most effervescent, her most affectionate, her most encouraging. When her mind danced easily, and she pulled us in as partners to her thoughts. No wondering, no worrying.

I sent a silent thank you to Mrs. Roosevelt.

Mama began: *"It is a truth universally acknowledged, that a single man in possession of a good fortune, must be in want of a wife. . . . This truth is so well fixed in the minds of the surrounding families, that he is considered as the rightful property of some one or other of their daughters."* She altered her voice to a euphoric British burble for Mrs. Bennet as that character said to her husband, *"My dear Mr. Bennet . . . have you heard that Netherfield Park is let at last?"*

I giggled at Mama's accent.

She laughed lightly in return. "Lizzy's mother is an absolutely delightful character, Louisa.

Such a brilliant bit of writing from Austen. Mrs. Bennet is infuriating, overbearing, and embarrassing, yet ultimately endearing because all her misguided actions are entirely out of devotion to her daughters' well-being. Austen is the queen of gentle—even bemused—satire."

One of the things I most love about my family is that no question is dismissed as stupid. Mama had always talked to us like we were scholars in the making. That had really taken with Butler. I wanted to show Mama that it could with me as well. So it was easy to admit not knowing the word and asking: "Satire?"

Mama kissed my head. "It's literature that shows us the foolishness of something by poking a little fun at it."

"Oh." I mulled that over. "What is Jane Austen satirizing?"

"Expectations of women." She smiled at me, waiting to see if I had a follow-up question. I didn't. "Shall we proceed?"

"Yes, please!"

We had just gotten to the ball scene where

Mr. Darcy declines to dance with Lizzy because she was only "tolerable" pretty and because he believed since other men were neglecting her that there must be something horribly lacking in her. Boys! But here was the wonderful part: Lizzy told the story of his snubbing her "with great spirit" to her friends with her "lively, playful disposition, which delighted in anything ridiculous." That sure enough showed up Mr. Darcy. The jerk.

I laughed outright at that passage. Mama was right. We were only ten pages in, and I was totally entranced. I turned the page for her to read on—but the phone rang.

As lucky as we were with Daddy's salary as a tugboat captain, we wouldn't have a phone at all were it not for Cousin Belle. She lives in Hampton, in its Victoria Boulevard historic district, a few houses down from Mama's childhood home. About twenty miles away by road from our farm in Poquoson—closer if you went by water. On account of that not being walking distance, or maybe because of her age and being alone, or maybe because of her attitude—Daddy called her all high and mighty—Cousin Belle had the telephone installed so she could reach us whenever she wanted. Only a handful of us in the county had a phone to ourselves. Most of our neighbors made whatever calls they needed to place from the general store in the village.

Cousin Belle called every Friday evening to hear Mama's report on the week's doings. The phone hardly ever rang other than that.

Mama's face turned white.

I darted to answer. "That you, Louisa June?" the operator, Mrs. McGrath, asked.

"Yes, ma'am."

"Your daddy is calling. Get your mama."

I felt my heart sink. "Is everything all right, Mrs. McGrath?"

"Oh yes, honey. Don't you worry any. He just wants to check in. He's on a ship-to-shore line connecting through the coast guard and the marine operator. Such a thoughtful man, your daddy. He knew your mama would be worried on account of Butler being along."

Being the operator who put calls through York

County's party line, Mrs. McGrath heard everything, knew everything about everyone. It was a good thing she was a God-fearing soul, Daddy always said, or she could blackmail the lot of us.

"G'on, Louisa," she urged. "Hurry now. Get your mama. Russell is bending the new rules for ship radio silence to make this call."

Mama was already standing beside me, trembling.

"It's okay. Daddy just wanted to say everything is good," I whispered, cupping my hand over the receiver as I handed it to her.

But it was Butler's voice that crackled through the line. "Mama?"

"That you, honey? Everything okay?"

"It's swell. Really swell, Mama. Daddy and I just wanted to let you know. You should come out with him someday, Mama. There's a wife on one of the barges we're towing. You'd love it. Dolphins splashed alongside us for miles. I could almost lean over the side and pet them! And the moon on the ocean—she slides her ivory ribbon through miles and miles of waves. It's gorgeous. It's . . ."

"Honey, did you say the ocean? I thought your daddy was going to take the inside route, up the Chesapeake, then through the Delaware Canal to the Delaware river on to Philadelphia."

"We ended up towing more than we thought, Mama. Three barges. Coal and lumber. And the company wants the cargo to move faster than it would through the canal. Don't worry. The sea is peaceful and beautiful tonight. I . . . I kinda love it out here. The reflection of heaven and clouds in the waters, the Milky Way so brilliant above . . . it's mystical . . . I started writing a poem, about stars in the waves . . . I'll tell you all about it when I get home. I love you, Mama. Daddy wants to talk to you."

Daddy's voice boomed. "All's well, Ruthie. You'd be right proud of him. He even survived Mackie doing his trick of sticking a knife into his cork leg, pretending it hurt. Butler didn't flinch a bit. He'll have great war stories to tell his classmates come fall. Gotta go—love you, Mrs. Brookes."

The line went dead.

"Don't that beat all?" We could hear Mrs.

McGrath wonder before she clicked off too.

Mama held the receiver to her heart before she slowly hung it up. "Stars in the waves." She smiled. "Doesn't that sound like Butler?"

I nodded.

"Let's both think on that image when we go to bed—that'll give us both sweet dreams."

⌖

People say life can turn on a dime, and as a waterman's daughter I've grown up knowing that tides and winds can shift without warning, hurling the innocent into wrath-of-God awfulness. But until you experience it . . .

The next morning, Mama was lively, actually singing in the kitchen, her heart filled up to happy with sweet dreams of stars and dolphins. Then we heard a knock on our front door. Mama opened it to a coast guard chaplain and lieutenant standing there—the people the military sends to tell a family that disaster has befallen them. The messengers of heartbreak.

I just can't talk about crying so hard I vomited

all over the preacher's bleached-white uniform. Or how the coast guard men had to carry Mama to her bed and give her a sedative that stopped her keening. How I crouched by her door while the sun moved in squares of gold across her bedroom floor, marking the hours passing until Katie made it home to pull me to my feet.

But I can recite the bare-boned facts of what those men came to tell us, if I squint hard and fold up my heart into a tiny steel tinderbox suffocating any flint of feeling. I can only do it so long, though, so here goes:

At midnight—when most of the crew was bedded down for sweet stars-in-the-waves dreams—my daddy's tugboat and its half-mile-long train of barges was chugging along the ocean side of Virginia's Eastern Shore, about halfway up its coastline.

Within plain sight of the little fishing village of Wachapreague, a Nazi U-boat rose up out of the moon-pearled waves. Fifty feet from the side of my daddy's tug. It opened fire. The first round ruptured the master cabin, destroying the radio equipment, so Daddy couldn't call for help. There was nothing for him to do but cut the barges loose so they could all try to make a run for it.

But the U-boat circled those slow-as-molasses barges, firing up the starboard and down the port side. Hitler's sub sank two of them within minutes. The third stayed afloat on its load of lumber.

Then the U-boat went after my daddy. And Butler. After a *tugboat*. Those Nazis fired repeatedly, blasting the engine room. Daddy's tugboat burst into flames and exploded.

All the people who'd been on the barges lived, clinging to the lumber, until a coast guard motorboat rescued them.

Of the eighteen souls working Daddy's tug, only two survived. They were being taken to the Naval Operating Base hospital in Norfolk, said the coast guard chaplain. Daddy was one. Butler . . . Butler was not.

THE
AFTER
OF IT

CHAPTER 6

addy lay in the naval hospital for several days—broken, barely breathing as nurses and doctors tended his burns—before he could convince the coast guard to bring him home. His Ruthie needed him, he said. But once he was here, our family doctor insisted that Daddy recuperate in my brothers' empty bedroom so he wouldn't disturb Mama's rest. She was so distraught she only managed a few hours of sleep a night, and then only with his prescription of laudanum. The rest of the time she reeled with sorrow.

For two weeks Daddy fought pneumonia that had come from the hypothermia of being submerged in frigid March waters for so long that terrible night. He had survived the Nazis hunting him down, the explosion that sank his tugboat, and clinging to a buoyancy ring from midnight to dawn, up to his neck in oil-slicked waves—all the while shouting Butler's name into the dark night and the flames, desperate to hear him answer. But once safe and at home, Daddy had nearly died again, drowning in congestion.

Katie and I nursed him through fevers and terrible delirium. The only thing that had finally cleared his lungs was Dr. Martin pumping Daddy full of sulfapyridine—a new medicine he said had saved a British commodore after the Nazis torpedoed his ship as well as a famous, much beloved lion in London's zoo. "What the heck," the doctor said. "It worked for the king of beasts. Let's give it a go." The serum worked.

Meanwhile, Mama had been drifting into the boys' bedroom at night to hold vigil by Butler's berth and books, usually around two or three a.m. Most mornings that was where I found her, huddled at the base of my brother's bed, finally collapsed in sleep, after hours of whispered mourning. She always seemed completely unaware of Daddy snoring in Will's bunk just across the room.

Until a few nights ago.

Daddy was finally well enough to stir out of his sleep when Mama had floated in like a shadow for her nightly Butler memoriam. When Daddy sat up and called her name, Mama lost what little hold of rational she had left. She was convinced Daddy was the angel of death. Mama started screaming, begging death to take her instead of her son. Daddy trying to calm her only made her agonized delusion worse.

Awoken by the shouting, I'd come in, running, just as Mama cried out, "I'll do it for you," pulling a pair of scissors from Butler's desk and preparing to plunge them into her own heart.

Daddy tackled her just in time. But then . . . oh, what she said next was so awful. Her haze of grief cleared, Mama knew exactly who she was looking at. She started shrieking, "You killed him," over and over, hitting and kicking Daddy, until finally she dissolved into his embrace, sobbing.

The look on Daddy's face—I hope to forget that someday.

c—o

Daddy took to the barn after that. I was carrying his meals out to him on a tray.

"Hey, Daddy, how are you feeling?" I greeted him as I put his coffee and hard-boiled eggs on the stool beside his cot.

"Better, thank you, Lou," Daddy croaked as he shifted and lifted himself up off his pillows. "How's your mama this morning?"

"Same." In bed. Washcloth over her eyes. Silent.

Sniffing in our mule's morning manure, I asked, "Daddy, why don't you come back into the house? This can't be good for your convalescing."

Daddy reached for his coffee, brewed "as strong as stump moonshine," just as he asked. He wheezed and grimaced as he fumbled with the cup in his still-bandaged hands and sucked in his first sip. "I don't want to set her off again. Besides,

I'm enjoying my late-night conversations with the ladies."

Daddy was sleeping in the stall right next to Cleopatra, our mule, and Athena and Hera, our two milk cows. Mama had named them, what can I tell you?

I watched Daddy chomp into a hard-boiled egg, taking in half with one bite. "I'm going to go pick some wild irises for Mama. I saw them starting to open up in the marsh yesterday. You okay until I get back?"

Daddy nodded as he chewed, thoughtful. "Thank you, Lou. You are . . . a . . . a mighty fine nurse."

"Thanks, Daddy." I smiled, bolstered. At least I was making some headway in trying to tug Daddy back to life. "See you in a—"

HONK-HONK. HONK-HONK-HONK.

"Louisa June? Where you at, child?" A voice shouted from the driveway. Cousin Belle!

Daddy grimaced. "Don't tell that bossy, bitty bat brain I'm out here, all right? Run along now."

He didn't have to tell me to run. I made the

quickest thousand-yard dash straight into that old woman's outstretched arms.

Her kiss was prickly. Her eyes behind those rhinestone-studded black glasses were so cloudy with cataracts I had never known what their true color was. Her wild gray hair was only so contained with tortoise-shell hair combs from another century. But leaning up against her polished 1930s Ford V-8 coupe—a high-octane, fancy car Daddy claimed only bootleggers had—Cousin Belle still carried herself with a jauntiness of a onetime handsome woman, who'd turned heads and didn't care a fig about the fact she did.

"What's up, darling?" she asked, her hand on my shoulder and peering at me from arm's length. "How you holding up?"

I shrugged and felt my eyes start to burn with tears.

"Right. Foolish question." She nodded, respectful. "Got some things for you and your mama." She tipped her head toward the backseat.

I opened it to see a dozen bags of sugar and just as many cans of Maxwell House coffee.

"They say rationing is going to start soon. Thought I'd stock you and me up." Taking my hand and guiding me in a slow twirl, Cousin Belle started singing the latest Ink Spots' hit, *"I love java, sweet and hot . . . Shoot me the pot and I'll pour me a shot, a cup, a cup, a cup, a cup, a cup!"*

I laughed in spite of myself. Then I jumped a little, as four pairs of big yellow eyes popped up at the front seat window. Cats. And some pretty disreputable ones.

"Oh, don't mind them. They were in the storm-drain gutter at the A&P. The bag boy loading the car told me they'd been living in there for a while now. He'd been giving them scraps. Poor things. So I just opened the car door, and they trooped right on in."

"Cousin Belle, you can't possibly need more cats." Last time I was at her house I'd counted at least a dozen lounging in the sun on her wrap-around porch or draped on the enormous wingback chairs in her library.

"No, I don't need them, child—but they

certainly seem to need me. Come home with me for a bit and help me clean them up. You can pick out some more books. I'll have you back in time to fix lunch. We can unload the sugar and coffee then."

I hesitated, looking toward the house.

"Bet your mama could use a good read." Cousin Belle's voice softened as she added, "And you too."

In her present state, there was no way Mama would read anything. But Cousin Belle's suggestion gave me an idea. Maybe I could read aloud to Mama—something funny, something new, something that might tether her to me for a bit and keep Mama from drifting away, out into troubled tides.

I climbed into her car, sliding those forlorn-looking cats over to give me some room on the creamy leather seats. Meowing in protest, they settled into one heaping mess of fur and whiskers at my feet. Cousin Belle revved the engine and gunned it, sending us lurching forward and racing away from sadness, for a few hours anyway.

Resting my elbow on the open window, I laid my head on it and watched my watery world whip by as Cousin Belle took us to the sole two-lane bridge that connected us to the outside. A pudgy little peninsula that juts out into the bay, Poquoson is embraced by the Back and Poquoson rivers, in between Hampton to the south and Yorktown to the north—cities framed by the wide, fast-moving James and York rivers. The Tidewater is a universe that shifts and pulses by the minute, with tides that seep deep into the land and rise and fall as much as three feet, four times a day, mixing salt and fresh water to create one of the world's biggest estuaries.

Pocosin was an Algonquin word, meaning "the Great Marsh." And that's what we are, a place that belongs far more to the hundreds of egrets and blue herons wading through the feathery inlets than to us. But humans come for the same reason those stilt-walking birds do—to fish and thrive. Perpetually flowing . . . thrumming with dragonflies, cicadas, crickets, katydids, mosquitoes . . . a thousand shades of green and blue . . . and so very alive. Butler had called it idyllic.

Butler. I swallowed hard to stop a swell of hurt.

There have always been dangers out in the waves—sudden, unexpected storms; jellyfish that float aimlessly during the summer in huge clusters that can instantly poison a careless fisherman; rivers that merge into one another with such fury the competing surges can spin and swamp a small boat in seconds. But nothing—nothing as malicious as Nazis lurking in the waves looking to kill.

Stars in the waves, Butler had said. Could I ever think that way again about the swells and breakers in the bay and the ocean beyond? That something beautiful and mystical, something uplifting, floated there.

I bit my lip and turned my gaze inland, away from the water where my brother had died. To the white frame cottages with picket fences Cousin Belle was whizzing by, swerving since she only saw so well, waving and shouting at people as we went. Family farms with roadside produce stands that would be full of vegetables for sale come August.

Miss Beulah's general store/post office/pharmacy. Ramshackle seafood packing houses. Skiffs tied to their piers, delivering their day's catch. Beached boats being scraped of barnacles.

Once we crossed the Northwest Branch Bridge to the roads leading to Newport News and Hampton, the vistas changed drastically pretty quickly. It's like a different planet. Especially as we reached the center of Hampton and its Victoria Historic Boulevard District—developed in the 1880s by a transplanted New York oyster magnate—where Cousin Belle lived and Mama had grown up. Turning onto a wide, magnolia-lined avenue, Cousin Belle swerved into her garage and wedged her car in beside an upholstered carriage from long, long ago.

She turned off the engine. "We need to name our new friends, so I can introduce them to the clan. Names that lend a bit of dignity to the hard times they've seen, a sense of destiny. Since there are four of them . . . maybe . . . Let's see . . . what about Aramis, Athos, Porthos, and D'Artagnan. What do you think, Louisa June?"

I knew this was a bit of a test. At Christmas, Cousin Belle had gifted me *The Three Musketeers*. She was fishing to see if I'd read it. I nodded to indicate that I knew exactly what she was referencing with her choice. "But those are *all* boys' names."

"Yes?"

I wasn't about to do the necessary inspection myself. "Do you know if these cats are all male?"

"So what if they aren't?"

"Well . . . . I don't know if a boy name is good for a girl cat."

"Pshaw, darling," Cousin Belle said with a chortle while opening her door. "One of the many things I love about cats is they don't care about that kind of thing." And with that, she lifted herself out, holding her door open for the cats to plunk to the ground one after another. Then they trooped right along behind Cousin Belle, single file, their mangy ole heads and tails held as high as if they were courtier-soldiers on their way to meet the king.

CHAPTER 7

I've witnessed many a strange thing at Cousin Belle's. But the sight of four soaking-wet alley cats sitting peaceably in a washtub as Cousin Belle scrubbed them, and a passel of other felines watching and yowling commentary, almost like—*you missed a spot there, lady*—was a wonderment.

"How did you learn so much about cats?" I asked as she plopped D'Artagnan into the old towel I was holding. I didn't even get the cloth wrapped up around him before he squirmed free, hissing at me, to climb up onto her shoulders.

"Now that won't do, young'un," she said, plucking him off and depositing him by her backside, where he sat dutifully, rubbing his head on her, leaving wet fur all over her shirt.

Watching the cat hair grow on her, I wrinkled my nose in slight disgust. "Have you always loved cats this much?"

"Lord love a duck," Cousin Belle responded emphatically, "no!" She pulled the next cat out of the water and this time wrapped him up tightly before handing him to me. "Now rub," she said. "Not too hard, but not too gently either."

She went to work on the third, flattening his big ears as she soaped up his tiger-striped head. "I couldn't stand cats before France."

"You went to France?" I gasped. "When?"

"During the war. The other war. I volunteered with the American Red Cross as a Gray Lady. Reading to the soldiers in the hospital, writing letters home for them, changing their bed pans and linens."

I wasn't exactly sure of Cousin Belle's age, but she was getting up there. Probably closing in on seventy. Which meant she was probably in her late forties or more when she made that trip across the ocean to a battlefield—a right bodacious move if you ask me. Most ladies that age I knew were focused on knitting sweaters for grandbabies and already discussing remedies for the rheumatism. I felt my mouth drop open in surprise.

"Don't want to catch flies, darling." She reached over and gently tapped my chin, leaving my face all sudsy.

"Were . . . were you afraid?"

"All the time." She smiled as she handed me the third cat to dry. That one—Athos—just hung limp as she passed him over. "But that's where I learned my respect for cats. Unlike other animals, they survived that Armageddon of man's making. All those trenches, where men hid and fired death across a no-man's-land at each other. Nothing but barbed wire and burned-out destruction.

"Mighty fine companions in such circumstances, those Frenchie cats. They hunted down all the mice around the hospital tents that might have plagued our boys in their cots as they recuperated." She tucked the fourth cat into her apron and rubbed it dry as she added, "I stayed on with the American Committee for Devastated France. Helped organize medical and social services at villages we rebuilt. That's when cats just started following me. Even straight to the train station when I was leaving to come home."

"Sounds like they wanted you to stay."

Cousin Belle *harrumphed*. "I wanted to stay."

"Why didn't you?"

"Well, I wanted a job of some kind. So I applied to a new government organization that later became the US Foreign Service. A friend and I both took the test and passed. President Harding recommended we be appointed. But the Senate refused. Its members thought it inappropriate that a single woman would travel overseas as a diplomat." She smirked. "My friend was able to mount a campaign of letters and telegrams, so she was eventually approved and sent to Switzerland. I just didn't have that support."

Cousin Belle stood. "I was devastated. But I looked for something else and ended up spending a good decade in Washington, DC, working for Congresswoman Rogers. I'd met her in the Gray Ladies as well. Working for her suited me better, frankly, agitating for all sorts of things, not just nibbling canapés and listening to self-infatuated ambassadors droning on at receptions. The congresswoman opposed child labor and fought for equal pay for equal work and a forty-eight-hour workweek for women.

"Right now she's pushing a bill for a Women's Army Auxiliary Corps to enlist women in noncombatant work as support for our troops. Wonder how those old congressmen codgers are taking that," she muttered. "Anyhoo, I thoroughly enjoyed what was an unexpected journey. Then I came back here," Cousin Belle extended her arms, "after having a good long adventure of my own making—which I hope you will do for yourself."

"Why did you come back?"

"The judge became ill."

The judge was her father and Mama's great-uncle, making Cousin Belle and me cousins-something-removed.

"And do you know," she added, "there were two cats sitting on the stoop when I arrived. Daddy had never seen them before." She held her hand toward me, wiggling her fingers, inviting me to clasp hers. She pulled me to my feet. "Let's go see about a good read for your mama."

❦

The four still slightly drippy cat-musketeers followed Cousin Belle into her enormous front hall foyer, big enough to have its own fireplace, settee, and armchairs, before a grand sweeping staircase. D'Artagnan—or maybe it was Aramis, I don't know, one of them—immediately sprang up onto the mantelpiece, knocking into a few silver-framed photos. One almost toppled off.

"Bon sang!" Cousin Belle shouted. "You, cat, will be disinvited from this house if you don't behave!"

The cat cowered.

She pulled him off the mantel, gently dropping him to the ground. "Behave." She held up a finger in warning. All four of the newcomers swirled around her legs in group-apology before settling into a huddle in front of the fireplace.

Cousin Belle lingered a moment over straightening up a photo of a sweet-faced young man in an old-timey sailor uniform. I figured Mama and I were related to him somehow, so I asked, "Who's that?"

"The boy I considered marrying once upon a long time ago. But he died on the USS *Maine* when it hit a mine. It sunk in Havana's harbor, starting the Spanish-American War." Cousin Belle paused. "I wonder what I read then that helped me. Hmm." She headed toward the library.

I wanted to look more closely at that young boy who might have won Cousin Belle's heart. Had everyone in my family had their life upended by hidden dangers in the ocean? But Cousin Belle was moving quickly, so I turned on my heel to dog her into the truly magical room of that house—the library.

We stood craning our necks, looking up floor-to-ceiling shelves. A rolling ladder ran along the four walls. "Jane Austen," murmured Cousin

Belle, heading toward an eye-level shelf.

"Mama already has those," I said. "I bet she has them memorized."

"Of course. Ruth read just about everything in this room before she went off to college. Let's see." She touched Dickens. Moved on to Trollope. Twain. All things Cousin Belle would have inhaled as reviving air in 1898, that Mama was sure to have already read in her English literature classes.

Twisting her mouth to one side, Cousin Belle chewed on her lip in thought—an expression I tended to make in class that I often was reprimanded for. I wondered if Cousin Belle had passed that on to me without my knowing it. She crossed the room to more modern-looking books, putting her face so close to read their titles through her sparkly glasses that her nose almost touched their spines.

She started pulling things from shelves willy-nilly, dumping them into the nearest armchair. Noel Coward plays, a collection of short stories by Dorothy Parker, a memoir by James Thurber, a collection of poems by Ogden Nash. "If all else fails, read her some verse by Nash. They'll make her laugh." Then Cousin Belle added fistfuls of magazines: *Harper's Bazaar, Vanity Fair, Vogue.* "That'll do. Now. What about you, child?"

I gazed up at the hundreds of books and then back to her pile. "I should probably just read these things to Mama."

"Nonsense!" Cousin Belle said. "You need some diversion and some mending, too, Louisa June. Hmm. I know you've read *Little Women.*"

Given my name and all, Mama had given me a special copy of it when I was christened. The cover was about to fall off I had read it so many times at that point.

"You are aware that she wrote other things?" Cousin Belle went to yet another wall of shelves.

"Sure. The sequels: *Little Men* and *Jo's Boys.* Mama gave me those, too."

"Oh, there are so many more than that. At least a dozen." Cousin Belle pointed to a shelf so crowded, there were books resting on top of books. "And not just novels. Short stories, memoirs, detective stories, gothic novellas." She put her hand on my shoulder. "Remember, child, a soul has many more stories to tell than just the one she is known for, or what people expect of her."

I stared at the row. *The Mysterious Key and What it Opened, Rose in Bloom, The Abbot's Ghost.*

Her voice was unusually hushed as Cousin Belle added, "You are actually quite like Jo March right now, Louisa. Telling your mama stories to keep her interested in this world, keeping her alive, like Jo does Beth. But I think"—she pulled out a worn, thinnish book titled *Flower Fables*—"that we should ask Miss Alcott to feed you as well. This is her very first published work, a collection of stories she wrote to amuse a neighbor's daughter. Delightful fables told by flowers and fairies. A little whimsy should do you good. Keep your mind in childhood, despite the . . ." Cousin Belle pushed her rhinestone cat glasses back up her nose, blinked, and smiled at me. "Despite the very adult responsibilities you face right now. All right?"

Again, I nodded, my eyes filling with tears a bit that she had noticed the terrible weight I was feeling, like a rowboat trying to pull a battleship out of a mud flat.

"Oh, and this." She pulled out a book titled *The Hobbit*. "This just came out four years ago. Wonderful story of a little person fighting evil forces to protect his homeland. Seems about right."

Gathering up the books and magazines for Mama, Cousin Belle tucked them into a woven basket along with the latest edition of the *Norfolk Daily Pilot*. Then she went into her vast kitchen to a gigantic icebox. From in between dozens of tuna fish cans, she pulled out four mason jars, filled with Brunswick stew. "I'm not the best cook, but it's nutritious. I thought you could heat it up easily to feed yourselves. A counterweight to all those fruitcakes, eh?"

I laughed—sort of. A dozen loaves had been left outside our door with little notes of sympathy. I knew it was because county ladies were proud of their personal fruitcake recipes, and it was an expression of respect for the recipient such a gift conveyed, given how long it took to make them. And because in early spring, dried fruit was about all that was left in their larders from the last harvest. I knew they meant well and thought a little sugar might lift our spirits. But a soul in mourning can't exactly live off fruitcake.

Cousin Belle checked the man's pocket watch hanging on a thick gold chain around her neck, reaching almost to her waist. "Time to return you."

CHAPTER 8

Back home, Cousin Belle sat with Mama for a bit as I unloaded her gifts of sugar and coffee, and tucked the bags safely into the pantry. Now that I was in charge of the kitchen, I'd need to remember to be careful with those supplies and to not waste a single grind or granule. Mama would have an even harder time lifting her head in the morning without a cup of coffee, sweetened just so. Daddy too.

I was heating up the Brunswick stew for everyone's lunch, when Cousin Belle came downstairs, shaking her head. "When does Katie come home?" She straightened up her glasses.

"On the weekends."

"You know how to use that telephone, right?"

"Yes, ma'am."

"I can be here in twenty-two minutes flat," she said, cupping my face in between her hands and leaning over so she could fully see and assess me. "I mean it now. I don't care what time, day or night. If you need me, I will come."

I nodded, feeling a little choke in my throat.

Cousin Belle tweaked my nose and kissed my head, strode out the door, and roared away down the drive.

I delivered some stew to Daddy out in the barn first.

"That cousin of yours gone?" he asked.

"Yes, sir."

He took a long inhale of the stew. "That smells mighty fine, Lou. If you work hard enough you'll become as good a cook as . . ." he trailed off.

"Cousin Belle made it actually."

Daddy froze, his spoon just short of his lips.

Then he chuckled, wheezed, and stuck it in his mouth. Nodding with approval, he swallowed. "Never look a gift horse in the mouth, eh, Lou? Even an ornery, high-and-mighty one, I suppose." He took another spoonful.

I smiled. Yes, Daddy was reviving a bit. I left him there with our mule and milk cows and went back to the house to take a tray up to Mama.

She just played with her bowl of stew, though, stirring and stirring, lifting her spoon, dropping it. "Cousin Belle's not that bad of a cook, is she?" I asked, trying to play off Mama's sense of politeness and family duty.

"Oh no, of course not," she murmured and ladled a spoonful of the chicken, lima beans, and corn into her mouth. She swallowed but then stalled out again.

This obviously was going to take a spoonful-by-spoonful coaxing. I pulled a footstool to her bedside and sat down on it gingerly. I always hated plunking my backside on the pretty sunburst of a daffodil she'd needlepointed on that stool and covering it from view.

Recognizing she was too distracted right then to really hear my reading a novel to her, I opened Cousin Belle's *Norfolk Daily Pilot* instead. I quick-scanned the headlines, looking for somethings nice to share. A wedding announcement, maybe. Or some witty column advice about how to cook the world's best pies despite coming war shortages. Or an interview with one of the Hollywood stars coming into Richmond to encourage our buying war bonds. I gasped a little—spotting what had to be the golden egg of somethings nice. Right there in the top fold: *Baby Born on Lifeboat!*

"Mama, look at this." I held the newspaper toward her, so the article was under her nose.

She pushed it down and turned toward the window. "You read it to me, sugar."

Amazed at what was being reported, I began:

LIFEBOAT BABY NAMED FOR RESCUE SHIP
Reported by the Associated Press.

NORFOLK, VIRGINIA, APRIL 11—The navy disclosed today that Mrs. Desanka Mohorovicic, wife of an attaché of the Yugoslav Consulate in New York, named her eight-pound baby son, born in a lifeboat off the Atlantic Coast, for the destroyer that saved them—Jesse Roper.

"Born in a lifeboat, Mama! Isn't that extraordinary?" I thought I saw her nod the tiniest bit, so I quickly continued to keep her attention.

Mrs. Mohorovicic, her two-year-old daughter, Visna, and twenty other survivors were crowded into a small lifeboat that had been adrift for two days in stormy seas after their cargo-passenger ship was torpedoed by an enemy submarine, just off Cape Hatteras, North Carolina.

In the rush to lifeboats, the *City of New York*'s captain had directed the ship's doctor, Dr. L. H. Conly of Brooklyn, to accompany Mrs. Mohorovicic. Eight months pregnant and struggling to carry her toddler, the young mother had fallen on deck and badly bruised herself. A young sailor gave her his life jacket and helped her onto lifeboat #4. The doctor followed. He clambered down a rope but lost his grip and fell hard, cracking two of his ribs against the rail, as the lifeboat dropped into a deep swell between waves.

Mama sat up off her pillows. "That poor woman," she murmured, a bit breathless. "The poor doctor." She waited for me to go on.

Mrs. Mohorovicic went into premature labor. In great pain himself, the doctor tended to her in pelting rain, total darkness, without anesthesia and only the simple instruments of the lifeboat's medical kit, as the boat pitched wildly in fifteen-to-twenty-foot waves.

The other passengers managed to stretch a sail across one end to give her some privacy and protection against the rain. Mrs. Mohorovicic "was awfully courageous," said able seaman Leroy Tate. "She never whimpered or cried. She had her feet in water the whole time. She was wet all over."

Thirteen hours later the baby was born.

A day and a half after the birth, the USS *Jesse Roper* spotted the lifeboat and rescued the survivors. Mother and child have been recuperating from the ordeal for the past week at the Norfolk Naval Base hospital.

"Thirteen hours of labor! Imagine," Mama whispered. "That's hard enough on land and in your own bed. What courage. And then to be adrift for another day and half without help. Good lord." She paused. "Was the father on board? Is he . . . is he alive?"

"It says here he was in New York City, Mama."

The baby's father, Joseph Mohorovicic, was translating dispatches that came over the embassy's Teletype machine in English, when he saw a navy bulletin that a woman had given birth in a lifeboat. An hour later he received a telegram informing him that the woman was his wife, and that she, the newborn baby, and his daughter were in good condition. He caught the next train to Norfolk.

The Mohorovicic family—father, mother, daughter, and the healthy infant—left today. The trip to New York was made by train because Mrs. Mohorovicic "never wants to go on water again."

"I would guess not!" Mama said, and then, miracle of miracles, she laughed.

I felt my heart leap up at her revival. Putting the paper down, I smiled at her as we both mulled over the astonishing story.

Imagine the range of things that had gone on in that daddy's mind, I thought. It was a wonderment that his head hadn't spun right around at such a tale of life or death for his family! Mine almost did just reading it!

Of course, the newspaper didn't divulge any of the sad stuff—but I knew that while that baby was coming into life, other souls nearby were leaving it, drowning in the convulsing waters. I couldn't help wondering what had happened to the young sailor who had taken off his own life jacket to give to Mrs. Mohorovicic.

My smile drooped a bit at that, and then I realized Mama's face had kind of frozen. Something harsh was working through her mind. "What night did the Nazis attack that ship, Louisa June? Does it say?"

It didn't, but I did the math, and my heart sank back down at . . . at the horrible coincidence.

Mama was working through it, too, because she gasped out before I could buffer the answer. "The same night . . . the same night they went after your daddy and Butler. The . . . the same night the Nazis killed *my* baby boy." She lay back down, pulling the covers over her head. Through the quilt I could hear her repeating over and over, *the same night.*

I cursed myself for being such an idiot. I should have read through the article and thought it out before sharing it with her. Assessed what the impact might be. My carelessness had only made things worse. There'd be no reeling her back in that day.

The same night, the same night, the same night.

Mourning my mistake, I considered the hundreds of miles of ocean that loomed between where my brother had been killed and where Mrs. Mohorovicic's ship had been torpedoed on the very same night.

Just how many Nazi submarines were out there?

CHAPTER 9

"You know the tides are coming in higher these days because of all them Nazi tinfishes floating around out there, right?"

"What are you talking about?" I pivoted in my seat to look back at my friend Emmett, who had come out on the water with me at twilight to scoop up glassy baby eels called elvers to sell for bait. Helping me out, just like Butler had suggested when he had thought he was only going away to college, not leaving me for forever.

"Everyone at the docks was talking about it this

morning—that the tides are higher and rougher because of the mess of U-boats Hitler has sent after us."

Emmett is one for half-baked conspiracy theories. "I don't think a bunch of submarines can make the entire ocean level rise, Emmett."

"LJ, you don't have no imagination, do you?" Emmett drew his twelve-year-old self up tall, looked at me with pity for my limited brain power, and tried to explain his higher understanding of the universe. "You ever take a bath?"

We were waiting for the sun to finish setting, when the elvers we were after would rise to the surface in little wiggly crowds. So I humored him. "Hmm, once or twice," I answered.

For a moment, Emmett's face turned into a right sizable frown, as if he were worrying about my house's plumbing. Then he guffawed, realizing I was pulling his leg a mite. "You is a clever wit. I never said different."

"Shh," I cautioned him. We were drifting soundlessly beside the reeds in our little tributary creek, where unsuspecting, youngster eels congregate, nibbling on the grasses named for them. Eels are friendly, inquisitive creatures and don't shy away easy. Not like minnows or crabs that take some cunning to capture. But they do dart away at loud sounds.

"Sorry," Emmett whispered. "In the bathtub, maybe you take a jug and push it down to collect water for rinsing your head? And the water rose up when you did?"

"Yes, but that's a bathtub, Emmett."

Shrugging, he ignored my disbelief. "Well, they're out there, LJ. Thick as sharks. I ain't gonna stand by and do nothing. I'm going to build me an observation tower and join the Confidential Observers."

"What's that?" I sat up, interested. I was dying to do something to fight Hitler, like Katie was, like Will and Joe, not just sitting and waiting for the next awful news to come from the sea. The only thing I was doing so far was pouring grease from cooking into an old coffee tin can, collecting glycerin for bombs being made by the Richmond Engineering Company.

"They were talking about it at the wharf," Emmett went on. "The navy's thinking on using us locals to help out. Giving our fishing boats secure radios to relay back to Norfolk safely, without all them Nazi spies picking up on it."

"What spies?"

"Have you had your head in a sandbank, LJ, like some ole ostrich? People are saying Hitler's got dozens of spies and saboteurs planted among us, breaking bread already. Going to our movie theaters. Buying ice cream sundaes at drug store counters. Keep a listen for any funny-sounding accents. I hear tell the police arrested a gas station attendant in Newport News last week and the varmint had all sorts of Nazi nonsense stuffed in his pockets." Emmett pointed at the water. "Here they be."

I jumped a little. Given all he was saying, I half expected a U-boat to be rising up right beside me. But he was pointing at eels.

By the light of the kerosene lamp we'd put on the deck of my family's boat, we could see green-tinted babies swarming just beneath the peaceful surface.

He dipped in his crabbers' net and brought up a pile of squiggly, dumping them into his bucket.

I did the same. In no time at all, we'd filled four buckets full of lively wormy fish, swirling around as happy as they had in the creek.

"Think that'll get us a whole dollar?" Emmett asked. We planned to take them down to Messick Point the next morning, where weekend fishermen launched, going out to the Chesapeake to look for rockfish and bass that were just coming into season.

"Dang!" Suddenly Emmett plunged his net back into the waters, jolting it around, calling on all sorts of angels, good and bad, to help him. I hurried to move the buckets up under the boat's cockpit, out of the way of whatever he was trying to haul up.

"I got you, I got you," he taunted the thing from below that was fighting him. Grunting, he yanked and whipped his net up out of the water, sending something dark and massive hurtling toward me.

Slimy wet struck my face so hard and heavy, it knocked me flat to the boat's deck. Something cold writhed all over me, trying to get its head down my collar, like my coat was an underwater reef that offered the thing safety.

"Eeew, eeew, get off me!" I grabbed at the sea beast, but it oozed out of my hands and slipped farther down my neck. "Eeew, eeew!" I tried to roll and get up and away, but the end of its long body was tangled around my knees. Despite my struggle, the baseball-sized head of the thing had quickly snaked along my neck and found its way down inside my coat and was squirming around my armpit. "Eeew, eeew." I tore at the buttons of my coat. Finally undoing it, I wriggled myself out and scrambled to my feet, panting.

"Why didn't you help me?" I spluttered, wiping off the lingering sensation of slime as I watched my coat swirl around, my assailant exploring the inside of my sleeve.

Leaning on the pole of his net, Emmett was shaking his head at me. "Ain't you never caught a full-grown eel before? She won't hurt you." He gazed at his catch proudly. "Look at her. She's a beaut. Gotta be four feet."

I had caught eels before, but I still shuddered, reliving four feet of guck sliding along my body.

"Hey now! Stop right there!" Emmett shouted at the eel. It had managed to find its way out of my coat through the wrist and was slithering up the edge of the boat toward escape. He pounced and nabbed it, holding the eel up with both hands, its long dorsal fin glinting silvery in the lamplight. "You got something with a lid, LJ?"

I pulled out another pail. But even after Emmett crammed the eel in and poured some water on her to keep her happy, she could push the lid up and off. He decided to sit on her for the short sail back to our family wharf.

As we putt-putted along the smooth-sleepy waters, Emmett thought things over and offered his eel to me. "She'd make a good dinner for your folks. Your mama can fix it up good."

The Powhatan people had loved eels, and they'd shown the Jamestown settlers how to stomp them out of the water for feasts. So they've been a Tidewater staple for centuries. And according to my brother Will, some of the Spaniards on his transatlantic voyages thought them a true delicacy, sautéed in olive oil and garlic. But Mama had never harkened to the concept, even as enchanted as she is with all things historical or European. "Mama's not cooking these days," I answered.

"Say what? Your mama's a fine cook."

"I know." I hesitated. "She's just not doing much right now . . . on account of . . . you know . . . She's . . ." I trailed off. I would trust Emmett with my life, but with Mama's? I wasn't so sure. He did love to gossip.

What would he do with the information that Mama hadn't gotten out of her bed for more than a month now? That she wouldn't eat and was growing paler and paler, like a gorgeous flower wilting before my eyes, no matter how much water I poured on it. The rumor mill on our little peninsula could grind a soul to pulp. Not that they meant it—well, not all of them anyway—but people do seem to love nothing more than dissecting and second-guessing a tragedy, laying out their belief that if *they* had been involved and in charge of things *they* certainly could have stopped it from happening.

Compound that with the fact Mama had never really been one of them, Daddy having imported her from Hampton and its old-Virginia circles. Her general melancholy and poetic nature were a bewilderment to them. She was considered "delicate" by the generous, "snotty" by the cruel, "an odd duck" curiosity by the rest. What would they say about Daddy hiding out in the barn so he wouldn't send her into hysterics?

So I stuck to simple. "She isn't coming out of her room much. She's in mourning." Anybody would respect that, surely.

"You're doing the cooking?" Emmett crinkled up his face in concern.

"I'm not that bad!" I protested. Our boat making it to the edge of my family's jetty saved me from thinking on the fish I'd recently fried that ended up as crusty and disgusting as old cow dung. We tied up and unloaded, putting the elvers into the outside root cellar until morning, when we'd take them to sell.

A bright moon and stars were already out, and Emmett would easily find his way home through our fields by their glimmer. He lingered, though, holding the pail that rattled with his eel, and looked at me a good long while before saying, "Know what my granny says?"

I steeled myself. His grandmother smoked a corncob pipe, and she never took off her apron or put away the small, thin knives in its pocket that she used to pick crabmeat faster than anyone in the county. Even as accustomed to the more outrageous local folk as I was, she gave me the heebie-jeebies.

"She says that crying never washes sorrow away, just makes it soggy and heavier to carry around." Emmett eyed me for my reaction. Not seeing an agreeing nod from me, he went on, in the same tone of concerned condescension he'd taken about the jug in the bathtub. "Granny would say that what your mama needs is a good jolt to get her going again. Like a tractor that's been sitting idle and rusting. Something that makes her jump up and take notice!" He thought a moment. "Maybe a fire in the kitchen?"

"What?"

"Just a little one that smokes and needs a swatting. You could shout for her help and—"

I cut him off. "That's not a good idea." Truth be known, I'm not sure Mama would budge for that.

"What if the hog got loose?"

I shook my head.

"What if you sprained your ankle—just a little—just enough to need some wrapping? Or . . . or what if your mule gave you a kick, just a bitty one enough to raise a lump. She'd have to—"

I shook my head again, interrupting his sermon. "You ever been kicked by a mule, Emmett? Don't think you'd do it on purpose if you had."

He mulled that over. "'Spect you're right." Cocking his head, he grinned. "I got it. What if . . . just outside her window tomorrow . . . I kiss you?"

"Eeew." I took a step back.

"Not a real one. Not a sloppy one. Just a peck.

Like this." Emmett stepped forward, his eel pail sloshing, but I moved quick to the side so his kiss hit nothing but air.

"LOUISA JUNE!"

I spun around. Daddy was standing in the barn door, steadying himself against its jamb.

Emmett chuckled. "Well, I got your daddy going, anyway."

"LOUISA JUNE!" Daddy bellowed again.

Turning on his heel, Emmett called back over his shoulder, "Night, Mr. Brookes," as he headed for our fields. In the crisp night air, I could hear him whistling "When You Wish Upon a Star" as he disappeared into the woods that separated his old sharecropper's cottage from our farm.

"Lou," Daddy commanded again in his captain's tone, a little less riled, at least, now that Emmett was on his way.

"Hey, Daddy." I approached. "You okay? Need some supper?"

Standing under a bare bulb that lit up the barn entrance, Daddy shook his head slowly, holding an envelope in one hand and some official-looking notice in the other.

My breathing snagged at the sight of official-looking papers. *Will. Joe. Oh God.* Please don't have done something to my other brothers. Please. "Is something wrong, Daddy?"

He held up the envelope. "Take this to your mama."

I hesitated.

"Take it." He rattled it, insistent. "She should deposit it."

Deposit. My heart started beating again. "What . . . what for? Who's it from?"

"From the tug company. For twenty-three dollars and twenty-five cents. Four days at four dollars. Plus a seven-fifty bonus for hazard pay. Minus twenty-five cents for President Roosevelt's new social security. For Butler."

"For . . . Butler?"

Reaching out, Daddy took my hand and pressed the envelope into it. Like we were playing a game of hot potato and he was desperate to pass it off.

The check felt like a fiery poker. But I grasped it, as ordered.

It scorched my soul. A check for Butler. Did the company think he was still alive? Or did its owners think that somehow that twenty-three dollars and twenty-five cents would make us feel better?

"What's the other thing you're holding, Daddy? That other paper? Are Will and Joe okay?"

His voice husky and shaky, he faltered as he tried to reply. "A report. On . . . the attack. The coast guard . . . the navy . . . the U-boat that sank us . . ." He cleared his throat and began again. "The coast guard and navy speculate that the Nazis were alerted to our whereabouts by . . . by my call to your mama. This is an official warning, issued to captains of all vessels leaving Hampton Roads, to keep radio silence from now on."

Then, without looking at me, Daddy abruptly shut the barn door, leaving me alone with Butler's check and the brutal, horrifying fact that a call home meant to reassure an anxious family that everything was all right with their loved ones—that kind of merciful phone call—could be intercepted by the enemy, listened to, and used to hunt down and kill the sailors who made it.

I couldn't move.

An owl hooted. Bats darted out of the forest for their nightly swoop and search, zinging around right above my head. Peepers started chanting in the pond.

I looked down at that check, fury burning through me. What was I supposed to do with it? Showing this to Mama might be the rock that finally, completely crushed her. What was Daddy thinking?

You know how to use that telephone? Cousin Belle's voice came to me.

Yes, ma'am. I knew. I'd use it after Emmett and I got back from hawking our eels. She could figure out what in the blue blazes I should do with the banknote.

But tonight? I felt my hand close into a fist that crumpled that check to my dead brother. The only reason Butler had gone out on that tugboat was the promise of earning sixteen dollars for the books he'd need for his college classes in the fall. A boy whose heart sang at the thought of poems and ideas. Suddenly I saw him grinning and reddening as Daddy teased him about maybe using some of that money to take a college girl on a date. Mama beaming when Butler shucked out a pearl from a dumpy gray oyster and gave it to her. Our kitchen full of life. His life.

With only the moon and the stars as my witnesses, I swore to find a way to fight back against the Nazis, to find a way to join those local boat owners out looking for enemy periscopes, and to avenge Butler.

And maybe . . . maybe if I came home a hero, having helped to alert the navy to the whereabouts of a German submarine and preventing that Nazi crew from sinking someone else's brother . . . maybe that'd be just the right jolt to get Mama living again.

CHAPTER 10

The next morning, after Emmett had harangued weekend gentlemen-sailors into giving us the kingly sum of sixty cents each for our buckets of eels, he and I sat on the dock, eating biscuits his granny had packed. Sixty whole cents. Emmett's mouthiness sure could come in handy sometimes. I munched happily, knowing I could buy a bottle of aspirin tablets to ease Mama's headache that had gripped her for days—and still have twenty-one cents left for other things.

The sun was rising, and the waves were still sleepy, gold-red from the dawn light. The peaceful scene should have mended my vengeful mood, but I'd awoken angry, a new hatred gnawing at my heart. I eavesdropped on the local fishermen shouting friendly jibes at each other as they loaded their deadrises for the day, wondering who could tell me for certain about the navy enlisting local boats to keep watch for Nazis. All Emmett could share that morning was, "Dunno. But I heard tell." Except for bartering, he was unusually quiet. Maybe because I'd told him that he'd know exactly how a mule's kick felt if he ever tried to kiss me again.

"Morning, Louisa June." One of our neighbors, Mr. Cooper, plunked himself next to me, making the pier quake. The fact Mr. Cooper could sail without capsizing his boat was the subject of many a joke around the peninsula. After he sat, I had a hard time telling where his belly ended and his knees began. His beagle wedged in between us—which required considerable wiggling—to sniff at my biscuit.

"Captain, mind your manners." Mr. Cooper shoved the dog back. "How your folks?"

"Fine, thank you," I murmured.

There was a long pause. I knew my family made the local watermen nervous. As strong a community as they are, they're also a superstitious lot, and our tragedy was no ordinary one they were accustomed to. The fact that death had risen up out of the ocean and gunned down my brother, for no good reason other than malice, rattled them. Almost like our bad luck could rub off on them. I'd first noticed the reaction at church, and then at the local hay and grain store. I was getting used to the sideways glances and the way people tensed and shored themselves up before speaking to me.

"Your daddy taking on a crew again anytime soon?"

I shrugged a little. "He hasn't gone out on the water at all yet. He's still shaking the cough from the pneumonia."

Mr. Cooper grunted. "Evil thing, pneumonia."

I nodded.

"How's Will?"

"Just left—" I broke off. *Loose lips sink ships* was the new slogan around the Tidewater—Uncle Sam's warning that any little dribble of details about a ship might find its way to the U-boats trolling along our coast. Like leftover bait tossed carelessly into the water that sharks detect and follow, tracking prey. Just like . . . I swallowed hard, thinking on the navy's horrifying conclusion that Daddy's ship-to-shore call might have alerted Butler's murderers to his whereabouts. I pressed my lips together to stop myself from saying Will was in a new convoy heading across the Atlantic toward England. "He's fine," I squeaked.

"Joe?"

"Training in Norfolk." That was safe to say.

"Katie?"

"Learning to weld ship hulls."

"What? You're fooling."

"No, sir. She's at the Newport News shipyard. She's going to help build Liberty cargo ships and a whole bunch of other stuff that . . . that I guess I'm not supposed to tell about." I thought on a new-fangled thing Katie had described when she was home last weekend, called LSTs—ships that could carry tanks and armored cars in their hulls and land them without needing a dock. Hinting at our boys making a beach invasion somewhere—using a thing my very own big sister had helped build. With considerable pride, I added, "She's doing her part, Mr. Cooper, to fight the Nazis. Speaking of which, I was wondering—"

"Well, I'll be darned," Mr. Cooper interrupted. "That girl's always been a pistol." He took off his cap to scratch his head before putting it back on. "Well, she's sure to meet a fine fellow there."

I started to say that was hardly Katie's reasoning, but I stuffed half a biscuit in my mouth instead.

Swinging my feet, I watched the shadows they cast on the water, dreading the next logical query—his asking after Mama. Dreading because I feared I might tear up, knowing Mr. Cooper's niceness matched his girth and that he'd be a sympathetic ear. But I could tell he needed to finish up his line of questioning before I could begin mine about the navy.

"So, how is—," he began.

"Is that Russell Brookes's girl?" shouted a gravelly voice. Mr. Cooper's father stomped his way along the pier. As lean as his son was meaty, the elder Mr. Cooper walked with a surprisingly spry speed considering how stooped with age he was.

Mr. Cooper winked at me and whispered, "That's why I was asking about your Daddy's crew. Pop's determined to join the Merchant Marine again."

"But . . . he's got to be . . ." I paused, trying to remain respectful.

"As old as last Sunday's fish fry?" Mr. Cooper asked with a laugh.

"Miss Brookes?" The older man bowed as best he could in an old-timey greeting.

I scrambled to my feet.

"Terrible tragedy," he said.

"Yes, sir."

"You tell your daddy something for me, all right?"

"Yes, sir."

"You tell him I'll ship out with him next he

goes. He'll need some experienced hands."

"Pop,"—his son tried to slow him down—"he needs *able* seamen."

But the elder Mr. Cooper waved him off. "What we need out there are some men with common sense born of being veteran sailors. You heard about those numbskull whelps on a merchant steamer the other night, thinking they saw a U-boat running on the surface, just off Norfolk."

The younger Mr. Cooper rolled his eyes, "Pop, they just panicked and—"

"Damn straight they panicked!" His father interrupted, getting agitated now. "They opened fire with a broken-down machine gun from the last war some nitwit put on board. Near blasted off their hands in a backfire. And what were they shooting at?"

"Pop—" Mr. Cooper nodded at me as if I could be shocked by whatever he was about to say.

But the elder Cooper was not to be deterred. "The idiots blasted one of our own—the USS *Dickerson*!"

I gasped. Joe had talked about the *Dickerson*

the night he announced he was joining the navy. "But that's the only destroyer out there patrolling to protect us," I said.

The old sailor nodded. "See, son, she knows." He calmed down from his ire enough to reassure me that the *Dickerson* was in port for repairs and the crewmembers who were injured were recovering nicely in the hospital. "But here's the kicker. That nervous-nellie steamer, what caused so much trouble, kept on going. Within two hours a real live Nazi U-boat spotted it and torpedoed it. Eleven tons of sulfur we needed for explosives to fight Hitler—gone."

He pulled from his pocket one of those official-looking handbills I'd seen tacked up at the village store. Most showed the Statue of Liberty urging Americans to buy war bonds. This one sported a determined old sailor, burlap sack over his shoulder, and a ship in the background. The headline: *You Bet I'm Going Back to Sea: Man the Victory Fleet.*

I looked up at his weather-beaten face and old gray eyes that had stared down many a storm surge, just as he now did his son. "Younger men need to go off to fight the Jerries. I can help take 'em supplies." He nodded at me. "You tell your daddy."

"Yes, sir."

Shaking his head sadly, Mr. Cooper lumbered to his feet as his father marched back toward dry land.

"Sorry, Mr. Cooper," I said. "I didn't know what to say."

"Shouldn't expect a young'un to fix something I can't manage to do as a grown man," he said with a grin. "Now should I?"

"I guess so, sir."

Mr. Cooper patted my head. "You take care now. Come, Captain." He turned for his boat, his beagle at his heels.

"Wait, Mr. Cooper?"

"Yes?"

"Emmett says the navy might enlist local boats to keep a lookout for Nazis?"

Mr. Cooper smiled. "Our friend Emmett is better than any ole news broadcast, isn't he?" Glancing toward the horizon, he said to Emmett, "Now if you can spread the word about the weather, boy, that'd be truly helpful. The coast guard is going to ban weather reports, worrying that information helps the Germans guess when our freighters might set off and where they might sail to avoid bad weather.

"We're gonna lose some fishermen to sudden storms for sure because we won't know what's rolling up and coming at us from the sea." Mr. Cooper scowled. "That's what we'll risk to stop Hitler. Meanwhile Virginia Beach stores and bars won't even douse their lights at night the way President Roosevelt asks, bellyaching it'll hurt their businesses. They don't seem to care that those Nazi tinfish can spot our tankers lit up from behind—by *their* boardwalk illuminated marquees—and shoot our boys as easy as a good-timer can a row of ducks at a carnival booth."

Again Mr. Cooper shook his head, this time with anger. "It's not as if their customers won't still come without all those lights." It took a moment for him to settle. "I'm sorry, Louisa June. I didn't answer your question. Yes, we got word a few days ago that the navy is going to form a civilian reserve, a Coastal Picket Patrol. Big ole motor yachts," he nodded toward the bay, "like those fancy ones you just sold your elvers to. Larger sailboats, too, fifty to ninety feet, that can go out to deep waters and patrol fifteen miles of shoreline for two days at a time. The navy may even give them a couple of depth charges to dump on the enemy's heads if they spot 'em.

"For us working fishermen who sign up, they'll equip us with secure radios so we can call back to the coast guard with anything we see." He scanned the waters leading to the bay, thinking. "They say the wake left by a periscope of a moving sub stretches a long ways, like an arrow point right to it. And the U-boats have to surface to recharge their batteries. We just need to be looking up from our crab pots to take notice." He turned back to face me. "You asking for your daddy? We sure could use him if he's thinking about joining this so-called Corsair Fleet."

"No, sir." I straightened up. "Asking for me."

Mr. Cooper burst out laughing. "Lord love you, child. That's no job for a girl. Especially one who must hope to someday be as pretty as her sister, I imagine." He paused, clearly weighing that possibility and deciding it came up short. "Besides, I suspect things are rough sailing at home right now. Your mama needs you." He pinched my cheek and walked away, chuckling. "Land sakes. Those Brookes girls—pistols."

I felt my face burn red.

"What'd you expect?" Emmett stood. "You *are* just a kid, and a girl, after all."

The only thing that saved Emmett from knowing exactly what *two* mule kicks felt like was his quick adding, "But you can help me with my observation tower. C'mon. I'll show you where I'm fixing to build it."

CHAPTER 11

We were passing the marshes where Butler and I had seen the swans, where he'd
dredged up that pearl, where I'd had my last real
conversation with my brother, when Emmett said,
all irritated, "You ain't heard a word I said."

Startled, my attention swung back to him.
"Well, you needn't get all swelled up like a puffer
fish about it," I grumbled, ruffled myself, having
lost the welcome sound of Butler's voice by Emmett
interrupting. "Just repeat yourself."

Emmett sighed and rolled his big puppy

eyes that I suppose a number of girls might find attractive. "My other idea is the old Back River Lighthouse. It gives a fine view of the bay."

"But how you going to get all the way there?"

"By boat." He grinned.

"You mean my family's boat."

He grinned again.

"Emmett, I can't be hauling you out here every day. I've got things to do. And they're sure to start rationing gas soon. Whatever we get for the engine needs to be put to fishing. Plus there is a thing called school, you know."

Not that I was giving the classroom much thought myself in the past weeks. I'd only been a handful of times since Butler died. Mrs. Parker was sending assignments to me. "You're way ahead of everybody anyway, honeybunch," she'd said. And I'd gratefully taken her up on studying at night on my own. If nothing else it kept away the loneliness of Katie being gone.

Emmett frowned. "Well, it won't be as good. I won't see as far. I might miss spotting a bunch of them Nazis." He wisely chose to stop short of saying because of my refusal. "But . . . I suppose . . . I suppose . . . my first place would work. Still up for helping me build a perch?"

I looked at Emmett blankly.

"You really ain't heard nothing, have you?"

Not really. Fuming about Mr. Cooper dismissing my volunteering for duty at the dock, haunted by the image of Butler so alive and hopeful at the oyster reef, I'd been engulfed in my own maelstrom of thoughts.

Emmett heaved a sigh so big he could have filled a small boat's sail with his hot air. "I was saying," he pointed across Back River toward Plum Tree Island, "I can build a little observation tree house there."

"But, Emmett, that's all salt marshes and floodwaters, scrub and cord grass. The mosquitoes will carry you off alive come summer. Plus in those narrow channels of fast-moving current a being can get all turned around or stuck in muck. Even if they know what they're doing—which you don't."

"You do."

"There's no solid ground to speak of."

"Is too. Right by the little finger of beach at Bells Oyster Gut. That's less than a mile from Messick Point. I already talked to Old Man Cooper about borrowing his log canoe. He don't use it no more. I can sail that on my own or row it if I have to. I already picked out a big, solid pine tree with branches thick enough to hold a plank. Just need to hoist some old fencing up, lash it to the branches, and then hang a knotted rope to scamper up and down. Come on, LJ. Help me out."

He could see I was faltering in my resolve to ignore his plea, because of my ache to do something, *anything*, to fight the Nazis. "Tell you what." He cocked his head. "Bullfrogs are just starting to come out. I'm beginning to hunt and gig them at night. I'll bring you a bucket of 'em every Saturday if you help me."

I hate fried frog legs. But Daddy loves them. And a bucket full was a dinner. I considered Emmett a moment and then turned the boat back toward Plum Tree Island. "Fine. Show me where you're talking about."

Fighting the incoming high tide waters, the boat popped up and down, jumping over the waves coming at it. It got worse the closer we got to the shoreline—a Tidewater phenomenon of shallow waters when being flooded with shifting currents. They can go from smooth to choppy in minutes.

I spotted greasy pools of oil smeared along the sand and reed grasses—and knew they'd been swept in from a tanker that had leaked its cargo, probably after being hit by a Nazi torpedo. My resolve to help Emmett grew.

"I see it!" Emmett stood on the bow and pointed. He jokingly mimicked the call of whalers: "Thar she blows!" A lone Virginia pine, tall and defiant, stood along a small strip of sand rimming the marshy island. I spotted an eagle perched on one of its higher branches, as if to prove what a good lookout it was.

Over his shoulder, Emmett grinned that goofy smile of his at me, his arm still up, pointing toward the island. I braced myself for his know-it-all "told you so." But instead, he whipped around, still pointing, but now inland. "LJ! Behind you!"

I turned. Two airplanes, small in the distance, were heading toward us, the buzz of their propellers growing louder by the second.

"They ain't . . . they ain't Nazis, are they?"

I felt a shiver of terror. But that couldn't be possible. No way. Not coming from the west. Could it?

I strained my eyes and caught sight of what looked like a smudge of blue on the side of one of the planes. I focused hard and was pretty sure that dab of blue was stamped with a white star. I kept watching, holding my breath.

Yes! "It's the Army Air Corps!" I called back to Emmett. "From Langley Field." Hopping up and down on my toes, all smitten and giddy with a patriotic crush, I clapped for what had to be a pair of flyboys lifting off from the airbase just a few miles from where we floated, right where the Back River split into two branches. I'd never seen any of them over these waters before. They had to be training to hunt down Hitler's subs. Thank God. I let out a long, relieved exhale.

"Hey there!" Emmett shouted as if the pilots could hear him, waving his arms over his head. "Think they'll see us, LJ, and dip their wings at us? Wouldn't that be jake? That'd be something fun to tell the old coots at the dock. HEY, BOYS!" he bellowed. "LOOK HERE!" He waved furiously. "HEEEEEERE!"

Suddenly Emmett froze. "What in the Sam hill?" His arms fell to his side. "What are they doing?"

The planes had been puttering along, not all that far off the water. But now they were climbing higher and higher, their engines churning hard, *a-ring, a-ring, a-ring*, and bucking the air as they fought to ascend.

Shading my eyes, I tilted my head back to look straight up to track them, the sun blinding me. I closed my eyes against the glare for a moment. So I didn't see the planes flattening out at cloud level and then turning their noses down—pointing straight at us.

But Emmett did.

"Turn the boat! Turn the boat!" he shouted, scrambling off the bow into the deadrise's belly. "Turn the boat!"

It only took a moment, I swear, before a hell-bent screaming was coming out of the sky toward us, as the planes dove toward the shoreline, winds scraping along their plummeting steel.

rrrrrrr-rrrrrrrr-RRRRRRR-RRRRRRRRRR.

The shriek grew deafening, and I fought the urge to cover my ears against it. I grabbed the wheel and pulled hard, turning the boat as fast as its old wooden hull could swing.

Ping. Ping-ping-ping. Ping.

Geysers of white spray splashed up all around us.

"They're shooting!" Emmett cried.

Ping-ping-ping-ping.

"Turn the boat!"

WHOOSH.

The planes zoomed past us in a blazing flash of sunlight ricocheting off their wings as they raced toward Plum Tree Island.

KA-BOOM!

An enormous volcano of water gushed up.

KA-BOOM! KA-BOOM. KA-BOOM.

The deadrise convulsed, rearing as exploded water shoved it up and over violently in a mini tsunami. I was hurtled backward, hitting the deck hard. Flashing stars punctured my vision. My head throbbed with a wild pain. My ears clanged. But I could see the boat's wheel spinning as the deadrise was whipped around by the surge. Its engine was spluttering and spitting, choking on the monster spray of water thrown at it. If it flamed out, swamped, and we ran aground in the shallows, the boat could have its bottom ripped open by hidden stumps of trees decayed and killed by tides and storms, lurking below the surface, spears of destruction.

I struggled to my feet. I staggered toward the wheel as the boat washed closer to submerged dangers.

Emmett was on his knees, shouting something at me. But I couldn't hear him over the high-pitched squealing in my ears, the thunder of my heartbeat pounding in my temples.

KA-BOOM!

I felt myself lifted and flung again, this time forward.

KA-BOOM!

My head slammed against the wheel, against the door to the deck below, against the floor.

And then the world went black.

CHAPTER 12

"Of all the incompetent ninnies. What did they think they were doing?"

I was swimming through a fog, thick as flannel.

"Classified? Classified, my rear end! . . . I see. Plum Island is being used for training?"

The voice was like the bell of a distant buoy clanging into the night, marking a safe channel of water. Beckoning. I followed it.

"What? . . . Blinded by the sun? Are you serious? Those idiots could have killed the child!"

That sounded like . . . like Cousin Belle. What was she doing out in this murk? I tried to open my eyes. But a needle of hurt ran through my head.

"Who is your commanding officer?"

I kept swimming, trying to reach the voice.

"He's busy? Oh, really? You best have your highest-ranking officer here within the hour to explain this to me. . . . Oh yes, young man. Here. Or you can expect a call from my very dear friend Governor Price."

Silence. Then footsteps, getting louder, approaching. "How is she?"

"Stirring a bit. She almost opened her eyes a moment ago."

That voice was Katie. I was sure of it. I tried to whisper her name. But nothing came out—like the haze of a bad dream, when you try to lift your arms but they're no longer attached to your body.

Far away something started ringing. Footsteps, this time receding, hurrying.

"The doctor just left. . . . Nothing broken. A black eye and a nasty lump on her forehead and a bit of a gash over her eyebrow that needed a few stitches. . . . Yes. A hurricane of a headache, but all right otherwise. . . . Yes . . . she's here. I sent a taxicab for her. . . . No, the shipyard was very understanding. . . . Yes. . . . What have you told Ruth? . . . I see. . . . Yes, of course. . . . The doctor gave Louisa June a painkiller for the headache and said to let her sleep and . . . yes, she's asleep now. . . . So why don't I drive them both home tomorrow morning? . . . Well, you could tell Ruth that Louisa wanted to borrow some more books and I asked her to stay overnight and help me with a few things. . . . Katie? We can explain Katie coming home once we're there. . . . Yes. . . . It'll be fine once Ruth can see with her own eyes that Louisa June is all right. . . . We are agreed then."

Footsteps again.

"What did Daddy say?"

"He sends his love. He hasn't said anything to your mama yet."

"That's . . . good."

Once more, I tried to speak, this time managing to murmur, "Katie?"

A hand took mine. Small but strong. "I'm here."

I felt another hand. Boney. "You're safe and sound, child. Rest."

Holding tight to those lifelines, I drifted off into nothingness again.

❧

Something was breathing on my face. Something was tugging on my hair. Something was pressing down on my heart. I felt myself sinking.

I fought against the darkness. I kicked. I thrashed. I lunged upward.

Yeowl. Hissssssssssss.

"Scat, you stupid cat!"

My eyes popped open. Well, one. The other felt all squinty.

"Hey there." Katie grinned at me. "That cat has been determined to check on you." She grew serious. "How are you feeling?"

I considered. "Okay?"

Thump. I felt something vault up onto my feet. D'Artagnan. He circled into a furball atop my toes, squashing them flat with his weight.

Sighing, Katie reached to grab him.

"It's all right," I croaked. "He can stay." Somehow it felt comforting to have a Musketeer guarding my bed.

Katie plumped and propped pillows up behind my back. I collapsed into them and turned to face her. She was still in her shipyard overalls and a bandana turban wound around her head, hiding her wavy hair.

Noticing my one-eyed scrutiny, she pretend-preened. "Ain't I purty?" she joked. "Cousin Belle pulled me straight off the docks. You know how she is."

I glanced around the elegant room with its high ceilings, half circle of vast windows, framed with fine-linen tasseled curtains and a wide, velveteen-cushioned window seat. "Where is Cousin Belle? I . . . I heard her earlier."

"Downstairs. There was a knock on the door. I expect some colonel is having the dressing down of his life." Katie smirked. "Those numbskull pilots are claiming they never saw you. That the sun blinded them. Evidently Plum Tree Island is their main target range these days for training in antisubmarine warfare. They were practicing dive-bombing and strafing and then dropping depth charges. You were in the wrong place at the wrong time, little sister. What were you doing there, anyway?"

"Emmett wants to build an observation tree house so he—" I broke off and sat up again. My head was still throbbing, but my brain was starting to work again. "Where's Emmett?" I asked anxiously.

"He's fine. He's home."

"How did I get here?"

"You don't remember?"

I shook my head and immediately regretted it as the motion turned the throbbing into pounding.

"Careful, Louisa. You had a heck of a smack to your head." Katie grinned. "Amazing the boat didn't crack open when your skull hit it."

"Hardy-har-har," I muttered.

"Emmett tried to scull the boat back toward Messick Point, but he got it all turned around so you two were adrift, swamped with water from the explosions, sliding southeast out into the bay.

As the pilots circled, all flyboy self-congratulatory, they spotted you and realized what they'd done and radioed back to Langley. The coast guard picked you up. Emmett told them to contact Cousin Belle. She told them to bring you here. So Mama wouldn't be frightened." She gave me a "you know what I mean" look. "Besides, Cousin Belle trusts her doctor more. And worried about their gigantic boo-boo getting out, the navy and the air corps were more than happy to bring you here rather than the hospital."

Swamped with water? Oh God. Had I killed our deadrise? How would we get by if I had? "Is the boat all right?"

"Oh yes." Then frowning a little with worry, Katie asked, "You don't remember giving the coast guard sailors what for about towing it in safely?"

"No."

"Well, you did. Pretty darn ornery about it, too, they said, even with your forehead all bloody."

Things were starting to come back to me. Like lying flat and watching the doctor's needle and thread going back and forth over my eye. I reached up and touched my forehead, feeling little wiry knots along my eyebrow.

"That shiner is a killer-diller badge of honor," Katie said. "Want to see?"

She stood and headed to a bureau, retrieving a monogrammed silver hand mirror. "Mirror, mirror on the wall, who's the fairest of them all," she teased as she held it up.

I couldn't help it. I gasped at my swollen-purple eye, the egg-sized lump on my head right above a crooked red gash held together with black stitches. Not that I was ever going to be as pretty as Katie, but this certainly clinched that. "That'll scar, won't it?" I murmured.

"Maybe. But that's okay." Her voice softened. "You look absolutely beautiful to me, Miss June-Bug." Katie's eyes suddenly shone with tears. "Because you're still here . . . and in one piece— basically."

Surprised, I smiled uncertainly. Katie was not usually sentimental, not about me anyway. And I'd never, ever, before heard her use Mama's nickname for me.

Katie put the mirror down and leaned over the bed on her elbows, to look up into my face. "You know, it's good for women to have a little . . . mmm . . . character in our appearance. Plenty of girls I'm working with do. I'm really proud to be among them. I feel so much more . . ." She paused, searching for the right word. "So much more myself than when I was worrying over my deportment for Mrs. Dawson at those dances. I have a purpose. Sure, the shipyard assigns us the least prestigious work—deep in a ship's hull, below the waterline. But that's where water might seep in if we don't do the job right. So we girls know that while our work may not be on display at the docks, we're what keep those sailors afloat and alive." She nodded to herself proudly.

"And character? Boy oh boy, do we have character. Our faces get covered with soot as we weld. By the end of a shift, our faces look like fryer chicken dredged in cornmeal. Everyone's breaking out in awful acne." She laughed—not with her usual easy, flippant mirth—but with an edgy snap. "They expect us to work as hard as any man to whip the Axis but still be calendar girls. We just had to attend a lecture about how to scrub our faces so our complexions," she cupped her hands around her face and fluttered her eyelashes, "as the speaker said, 'remain their most pleasing.'"

"Oh, you're always beautiful," I said. "No matter what." I wondered what they'd say about my complexion, which had become a bit argumentative with me of late.

Katie smiled. "You know, Emma's eyes look a lot like your shiner right now. She got hurt on our shift. Our helmets have shields that we pull down as we melt and seal the metal—to protect our eyes from the fire. But we work packed tight, every six feet. If you lift your shield to get a little drink of air and the girl next to you fires up her torch and you don't quick look away, her flash scalds your eyes. They can be sore and swollen for a week. Emma's been in our room for days now with compresses over her eyes.

"Oh! Sorry. That reminds me." Katie gently put a wet washcloth over my eye.

The cool felt wonderful. I waited for her to go

on. These were the kind of big sister confidences I'd so longed for with Katie. But she'd quieted, thoughtful, a stillness that was unusual for her.

"At least Emma was doing something to fight the Nazis," I murmured. "Like you are. This was just a dumb accident. I'm not doing a thing to help."

"Oh, honey, that's not true. You're helping Mama, after . . ." Katie stopped, sighed, and looked down at the floor. "After Butler."

A long moment passed before she took my hand and kissed it, giving me a more typical Katie, devilish look. "I know how you've contributed to the war effort. You just reminded pilots and navigators and bombardiers to take a good look before dropping bombs. And that they all need to wear their sunglasses! They will look far more debonair that way too!"

I managed a hint of a giggle.

e~ว

There was a knock on the bedroom doorframe. Cousin Belle was standing in it, shadowed by a very chagrined-looking Army Air Corps lieutenant colonel, his hat in hand. "You're awake!"

"Yes, ma'am," I answered, sitting up.

"Excellent. This young man has something he wants to say." She pushed her glittery cat glasses up her nose, crossed her arms, and peered at him. "Isn't that right, sir?"

The officer cleared his throat. Then he startled as Aramis and Athos suddenly, silently appeared to swirl around his legs while Porthos started sharpening his claws on the man's pants leg.

"Come, come, sir," Cousin Belle said. "Speak up."

Trying to ignore Porthos climbing up his crisp-pressed khaki pants by his claws, the officer said, "I've been sent to apologize for the incident. And . . ." Porthos had made it to his waist. The officer looked down, befuddled and jittery.

Not bothering to hide her amusement, Cousin Belle plucked the cat musketeer off the man. "Go on."

"Yes, ma'am." He tugged his uniform coat down to realign its starched fit. He looked back at me. "As I was saying, to apologize and to ask if your nation can count on you to not mention the encounter? Public knowledge of our training program might endanger its success."

Katie snorted. "Encounter?"

Athos started sharpening his claws on the officer's pants leg. Aramis joined in on the other leg. Cousin Belle did nothing to help him.

We all watched the man squirm. Of course I wouldn't blab about our nation's training programs against the Nazis and somehow endanger them. What kind of a crowing ninny did he think I was? I felt my face get hot with righteous indignation. I was as much a patriot as he was, even if I didn't have a uniform . . . or official welder jumpsuit-overalls like Katie. But I was unsure what I had a right to say.

Watching me closely, Cousin Belle offered this. "Louisa June, when your friend Emmett was asked the same thing, evidently his answer was if he was a confidential observer, he wouldn't have time to be jabbering about anything. It seems the air corps is starting to train civilian plane spotters to identify aircraft by their underbellies—as a warning system against any Axis planes that might come. Emmett will receive that training."

I smiled. Yessiree, that boy's mouth came in handy.

Seemingly as relieved as I was, the officer asked, "Would you be interested in the Aircraft Warning Service as well, Miss Brookes? Not to reveal too much, but age doesn't matter. Teens can participate in what we're calling the Ground Observer Corps. You have to memorize eighty-some different plane silhouettes—Allied and Axis. Plane spotters could potentially be critically important to our defense."

Were we really worrying about an air invasion from Hitler? I chewed on that for a moment. Given Pearl Harbor, any horror was possible, I supposed.

"You were looking for a way to help. Do it for Butler?" Katie whispered to me.

Butler. My heartbeat tripped on itself. But Butler had died at the hands of Nazis in the waves, not the skies.

I assessed the officer, who was managing to stand still while both Aramis and Athos used him as a scratching post. I'd give the man respect for that much at least.

"What about the Corsair Fleet?" I asked.

The officer blanched. "I . . . I have not heard of such a thing, miss." He paused. "But . . . *if* such a volunteer force existed, I am certain the navy would require expert, experienced, adult boaters."

Annoyance boiled up in me. "So you're saying you're concerned about spotting Nazi planes that are very unlikely to reach our shores but not about the U-boats that are here already and taking down ship after ship?"

"Of course not," he blustered, "that's exactly what those planes you saw are . . ." He broke off and recalibrated himself. "What they are preparing for as a . . . a possibility."

"Possibility?" Katie and I exploded at the same time. I knew the navy was downplaying, even trying to hide, the news of U-boat attacks to prevent panic. But how ridiculous could this officer be?

"You do know how our brother was killed?" Katie near shouted.

"Yes, miss. I'm sorry."

That's it? That's all he was going to say?

Katie got ahold of herself first. Clearly working those hulls was teaching her how to better deal with rule-happy authority. Her voice reeked with fury at the man sticking to impersonal, official doubletalk, but she kept herself polite. I'd have to remember how she did that. "There's nothing to stop my sister from keeping an eye out, is there, Colonel, while she's *expertly* navigating those waters to fish?" she asked.

"No, miss."

"Or for hightailing it to a radio to give you some information if she sees something?"

"No, miss. Nothing to stop that."

"Well, then." Katie smiled at me, raising her eyebrows in a sign of: *Your turn, little sister.*

"Well . . ." I murmured. "It would seem to me . . . that I better make sure our deadrise is as bay-worthy as possible." As my thoughts gelled, my voice quickened. "Has anyone gone over it carefully to make sure it's all right after the . . . ?" I tried to remember the euphemistic word he'd used.

"The *encounter*," Katie provided the word, anchoring it with sarcasm.

My memory darted along our boat, recalling spots of peeling paint, the engine's mechanisms looking a tad rusty. "Oh yes, the *encounter*. That flooding probably waterlogged some decking, might even have gummed up the engine a mite."

The officer smiled. "I know some people who could check on that," he said. Shaking off the cats, he nodded to Cousin Belle, put his uniform hat back on, and headed for the stairs.

After seeing him out, Cousin Belle returned, carrying a tray with soup for me. "Ladies," she began as she put the tray across my lap and sat on the end of the bed. "That was quite the negotiation you just conducted. Worthy of the best bill-conferencing I ever heard on the Hill in the service of the congresswoman. I'm proud of you." She reached out and gently waggled my toes under the blanket. "But please let me clarify one thing, child. When I suggested you have adventures of your own making, I didn't really mean making yourself target practice."

CHAPTER 13

After I finished my soup, Cousin Belle gave me one last pill the doctor had left to ease the pounding in my head. I slipped off to sleep again. So it was around twilight when I awoke to Katie gently shaking my arm.

"There's word that a U-boat has been sunk and that the navy is holding a secret burial of its Nazi crew tonight at Hampton's National Cemetery. Cousin Belle's grocery boy told me. About a fifteen-minute walk from here. I'm going. It . . . it could be the crew that sunk Daddy's tug, the men who killed Butler. Want to come? Think you're up for the walk?"

I got up out of that bed and into my clothes in two minutes flat.

"Should we tell Cousin Belle?" I asked.

"She's not here. A neighbor called to say a cat got stuck up her chimney somehow and asked her to come help," Katie answered. "That's why we can't drive." She took hold of my arm gently. "You sure you're okay to do this?"

"Positive."

We found our way down the street past the Hampton Institute to the cemetery as dusk fell and street lamps began to snap on one after the other. I winced a bit as each bulb glowed to life, thinking about Mr. Cooper damning the merchants in nearby Virginia Beach for insisting their lights stay on for business. We were right on the edge of the bay here, right where the James River widens to enormous and joins waves with its little sisters, the Nansemond and Elizabeth, to gush into the bay and surge toward the Atlantic. Right beside the little Hampton River as it splashes in to join them like a toddler chasing after older siblings.

These streetlights would skip bright across all that water, backlighting any freighter leaving Hampton's port as clearly as a shadow puppet, making it an easy target for any Nazi sub lurking by the bay opening. I couldn't believe the city officials weren't dousing them.

Snippets of alarmed conversation bobbed alongside us as we joined the shoal of Virginians rushing toward a chest-high brick wall edging the cemetery.

Nazis? Burying Nazis? Where did they come from?

Were they saboteurs? Assassins maybe?

What if it's a scouting expedition—for a land invasion?

What if there're more of 'em?

One voice blared louder than the others. "I'm telling you, we should be heading home and loading every rifle we've got," warned one man as he and a companion bustled past us.

"But we bagged these guys," his friend corrected him. "This is good. We got their U-boat."

"How do you know that?" the first man countered. "The navy hasn't announced anything. There's no official word of any kind. I only heard tell of this funeral because our cook's son helped dig the graves."

"Well, I've got a buddy at the Norfolk Navy Base and . . ." His friend lowered his head and his voice so I couldn't hear the rest.

Katie put her arm around my shoulders to hurry me along. "Let's get closer to that man. If he has a friend at the base, he'll know some actual facts."

We hustled to keep up.

"It was that old rust bucket, the USS *Jesse Roper*, what sunk it," the man was still talking as they came to a stop, melding into the mass of people, three deep, already packed up against the cemetery's wall to peep over it into the graveyard.

"The USS *Jesse Roper*," I whispered to Katie. "That's the World War I destroyer that found the lifeboat baby."

"The what?" She looked at me, puzzled. "Never

mind. Tell me later." Katie tugged on the man's sleeve. "Sir?"

He turned, startling as he saw me. "Goodness, girl! What happened to you?"

"Fishing accident," Katie answered for me without missing a beat. "Did you say you have a friend at the base?"

Hearing her question, about a dozen people encircling us swung round to listen. *Shh-shh* a hush rippled back through them. *This man's from the navy. He'll know what's up.*

"Now you done it," the first man muttered.

His friend squirmed, looking around at the hushed faces. "I really shouldn't say." He tried deflecting attention from himself. "And you really shouldn't be worrying your pretty little head about this, miss."

Even in the gloom, I could see Katie's face flare furious red as her whole body tensed. Somehow she managed to keep herself civil so she could get the information she wanted. How many times had Mama gently corrected Katie's wayward heart by saying, "You'll catch more flies with honey than vinegar." Not that Katie should conform or accept wrongs, mind you. All Mama meant was that remaining polite was a way to spark a more satisfying conversation, the difference between a simmer and a flash-fry.

This man was most definitely a fly. And Katie threw him a honeycomb.

"Well, sir," Katie began, "I am worried, you see, for our safety. For all of us," she nodded toward her listeners. "I and my little sister here," she pushed me forward a bit and waited for the collective gasp of the circle around us once people got a load of my banged-up face. "We want to know if these are the Nazis who killed our brother. Circling and blasting our Daddy's tugboat—a little tugboat—until it exploded. Our brother . . ." She choked up a little at that, no playacting. "My little brother was only seventeen."

A murmuring went through the people around us. *What did she say? A tugboat. Why would they go after a tugboat? Good Lord—that might mean they'd go after a fishing boat. Look, look. Look at that child's face—did she say the Nazis went after her?* More bodies turned around and pressed toward us.

I reeled—not from their stares but from their questions. These people didn't know about Butler? I knew the city folk of Hampton were weirdly detached from our way of life just across Back River, but still. How could they not know? My world had stopped spinning, suspended in horror when we got word about Butler's murder. How could these people not even know?

I felt Katie patting my shoulder. So I took a deep breath and another step forward and looked as pitiable as I could—which wasn't hard, considering. I made my voice all quivery, which also wasn't hard. "Please, sir . . . do you think this might be that crew? I . . . I think I'll rest easier knowing they are in the ground and no longer out there." I gestured toward the bay.

Would I, though? Would I ever?

The man hesitated.

The circle pressed in closer.

"If you know anything about them," I coaxed. "Anything at all?"

With all those eyes on him, all the anxiety rising up into the air like the damp of twilight, he
relented. "All I know, honey, is that they recovered twenty-nine bodies from the sea after a battle
with the *Jesse Roper*. No survivors. They brought
the bodies back to base and searched them for
information—notes, photos, that kind of thing.
My buddy said what they did find identified them
as being the crew of U-85. That's all I know. Nothing about . . . no information about the sub's prior
activities. Not that I know of. I'm sorry."

U-85. Did that mean there were as many as
eighty-five German submarines out there, treading
water, lying in wait? I could see the fear of that
same question wash over the faces of the people
staring at me.

De-tail, fall in!

From the other side of the wall a military-brisk
voice shouted.

At-ten-tion! There came a responding click as
soldiers snapped to attention. *For-ward—march!*

The crowd pressed back toward the wall. Katie
and I winnowed our way in closer, people who'd

heard our story making way for us. We reached the brick fence in time to see a slow-step parade of army soldiers carrying more than two dozen plywood caskets, eight men around each coffin. To the side stood a delegation of army and navy officers, plus a naval honor guard ready to fire a salute.

"What the hell," muttered the man who'd wanted to go home to load his rifles—as if he could protect the continent against an invading Nazi army with his hall closet duck-hunting arsenal. "They're giving these SOBs full military honors."

"Well, they are sailors, under orders, serving their nation," his friend whispered back. "It's the honorable thing to do."

"Honorable," Katie muttered. "Honoring men who attack civilian ships from hiding, without warning?"

A few people around us echoed her grumbles.

The pallbearers marched to their assigned gravesites, marking time until the final coffin reached its place.

Halt!

They lowered the caskets to the ground.

Let us pray. A chaplain began the service.

Out of habit, I bowed my head and closed my eyes at those words. That was a mistake.

Taking my gaze off the scene in front of me let my mind's eye hurl me back to Butler's funeral. The mist of cold rain. The scent of dug-up dirt that before had meant the promise of planting new life each spring and now would just smell of death to me. The minister's words over my brother's casket so hollow—as incomprehensible as the brays of a mule. Mama collapsing to the ground, as if she would crawl into the grave with her baby boy.

And that awful *thunk*. The *thunk* of a clod of earth that burial tradition required I toss down on my brother. *Thunk*. A wad of dirt imprinted with my heartsick, white-knuckled grasp. *Thunk*. Knocking on the lid of his casket, just as I used to do every morning on his bedroom door, knowing he'd open it up and greet me with that sunshine of a smile. "Hey, Louisa June, what's up?" *Thunk.* That horrible moment when I realized my brother would never answer any knock from me again.

Because of a bunch of Nazis hell-bent on taking down a little tugboat.

There'd been no honor guard at Butler's funeral. No lineup of officials to mourn him. No acknowledgment at all except a check for twenty-three dollars and twenty-five cents, which included a seven-fifty bonus of hazard pay. *Hazard.* Seven dollars and fifty cents compensation for being attacked by Hitler's Reich. Seven dollars and fifty cents for my brother's life.

No, I breathed. No, no, no, no.

I honest to God don't really know what happened next. I must have been shaking my head as wildly as a dog stung by a bee because I could feel a wild clanging of that headache against each side of my head. *No, no, no, no.*

"Louisa, hush."

No, no, no, no. Clang, clang, clang, clang.

"Louisa!"

I felt cool dirt in my hand. An ache in my arm. Another wad of earth. Another ache. Another and another.

"Louisa! Stop throwing dirt!"

No, no, no, no.

"Move away from the fence, miss." A low, authoritative voice, slightly threatening.

"Yes, sir. Come on, Louisa, we're leaving."

No, no, no, no.

"Louisa!"

No, no, no, no.

I felt my feet stumbling, dragging.

No, no, no, no.

"Louisa June, honey, stop it." Hands were on my shoulders, shaking me gently.

I tried to push them away.

"June-Bug!"

Mama?

"June-Bug! Look at me. Look . . . at . . . me."

I focused. It was Katie. Katie searching my gaze. Tears on her beautiful face.

"There you are." Katie grabbed me into her

arms and hugged me hard. "Don't be like that. Please don't be like that."

And without her having to say it, I knew what my sister meant. Don't be like Mama.

I had just taken a nosedive into Mama's world of despair, her disconnect from the reality around her when she could no longer fight her demons. For just a moment. And it was terrifying.

CHAPTER 14

B ack at Cousin Belle's, Katie explained what had just happened at the cemetery as we sat across from her in the old whitewashed benches beside the kitchen table. One by one, Aramis, Athos, Porthos, and a half-dozen other cats came in and joined us, filling up the cushioned seat beside me or whirling around Cousin Belle's feet. I fleetingly wondered where D'Artagnan was. He'd seemed so insistent on being with me earlier in the day.

Cousin Belle nodded solemnly as Katie told about the dead Nazis, that they were crewmembers of a U-boat our navy had managed to sink, the military honors given them, and then the fact I had suddenly started flinging mud balls at a bunch of dead guys.

"I . . . I don't think she realized she was doing it," Katie ended.

I wanted to remind Katie I was sitting beside her and that it wasn't polite to speak about someone who was right there. But under the circumstances of my barely avoiding being arrested by an MP, I remained quiet.

Holding up her index finger in a just-a-moment gesture, Cousin Belle stood, saying, "I think we need a little sustenance before going on." She went to her massive icebox and retrieved a bottle of milk, which brought all the cats running. "Not for you, my friends, shoo." In a large pot, she poured in milk, to which she added several split vanilla pods and a large dollop of honey. Then she grated in nutmeg and cinnamon. Percolating, the spices filled the kitchen with a comforting, delicious aroma. Smells we couldn't often afford in our house.

After a few minutes of staring thoughtfully into

space while slowly stirring the milk so it wouldn't scald, Cousin Belle poured the elixir into three bone-china teacups. She brought them back to us. If I weren't so upset, I'd have felt like Sara in *A Little Princess*.

She sat down, blew on her warm milk to cool it, and eyed me over the rim of her teacup. "Sooo," Cousin Belle said dramatically and with a wry smile, "I'm not sure you understand what I mean by adventure, child."

I laughed a little in spite of myself. Katie too.

"Although, I have to say—throwing dirt clods at the enemy is something I might have done had I been there with you. Here we are again, the very same people fighting one another. And again, using sinister methods that ignore any kind of morality. I'm pretty damn angry myself."

"Really?" I asked, shocked. "You always seem so . . . so . . ."

"Diplomatic," Katie provided.

Cousin Belle guffawed, and I caught a glimmer of the irreverent middle-aged woman who'd stride into a field hospital and offer her help.

"There is a difference between anger and hate, child. Anger at this war, anger at the men who shelled your daddy's tugboat and the officers ordering that kind of attack, anger at people who'd follow a monster like Hitler?" She shrugged. "It's hatred you really want to fight off, child. Hatred is poison." She sipped on her milk.

I mulled over her words and thought of one of the Louisa May Alcott books she'd lent me. "You know that collection of *Flower Fables*?"

"Yes," she answered slowly, clearly puzzled by my segue. But she played along. "Are you enjoying the stories?"

"There was one story in it that plagues me a mite. Elves shrink a human child to their size and take her to a fairy hospital—where they nurse flowers injured by human carelessness. The elves tell the human girl that"—I could repeat it exactly because the words tugged on my conscience and made me feel guilty for my feelings, the way a sermon at church could—"that 'love and gentleness, uncomplaining forbearance of troubles, helped heal and revive the hurt blossoms.'"

"Oh, I see where you are going with this now." Cousin Belle let out her breath in relief. "For a moment, I was a bit concerned about that bump on your noggin affecting your train of thought. Forbearance, love, and gentleness—that sounds all well and good, and certainly are traits we are supposed to strive for. But . . . that's a lot to live up to, isn't it, child? Given the circumstances."

I nodded.

"That's not really what I am talking about." Cousin Belle looked at me carefully. "Let's try this reference instead. Because honestly I think Louisa May Alcott struggled with this herself. Do you remember the scene in *Little Women* when Jo says that sometimes when she's in a passion, she gets so savage she could hurt anyone and enjoy it?"

I did. I'd been a bit shocked by it.

"Do you remember what Marmee says to her?"

"Mmm . . . that she had just as bad a temper."

"*Exactement.* And what next?"

"I . . . I can't remember."

Cousin Belle smiled. "Marmee says that after forty years of trying hard to control her temper, she was learning how to not let it get the better of her. That's the key, to not let anger get the better of you. To not let anger *rule* you."

My eyes well up a little.

"What else are you thinking, Louisa June?" she asked gently.

I was too afraid to put words to it—that saying so made it so.

"She's afraid she's like Mama," Katie blurted out.

I couldn't help but look harsh at my sister for that.

"Well, you do, don't you?" she countered. Then she admitted, "I worry about it for myself sometimes. Sometimes I get so sad. About Butler. So sad. It . . . scares me."

Katie? Vivacious Katie? The pistol of Poquoson? Katie felt like that, too?

Wide-eyed, we both turned to Cousin Belle.

"Sorrow is a different thing, ladies." Cousin Belle put her teacup down. "Here's what life has taught me about that. I have felt sadness so sharp that it has knocked me to my knees—literally—and made it almost impossible to breathe. For days. Even weeks. That's grieving. That's normal when you've had a terrible loss or shock.

"My advice on sadness is to not ignore it, not dismiss it. Stare sorrow straight in the face. Recognize the pain for what it is. Then it will back down a tad and walk beside you, maybe give you a little bit of a limp for a while, or for forever. But it will not undo you or sneak up on you from behind in a surprise attack. Of course, doing that—facing sorrow head-on and accepting its presence as an unwanted but tolerated companion—takes honesty, courage, and a bit of spit. Which you both have in spades," she added with a raised eyebrow and fond teasing in her voice.

She paused to let that really sink in. "Now here's the thing about your mama. She's grieving right now. But it's worse for her, because she suffers melancholia or what more doctors are calling depression. That is very different from being sad. It's a darkness . . . a flatness . . . a sense of foreboding, a . . . an *ennui*."

"What?" Katie and I spoke at the same time.

"*Ennui?* Feeling that nothing has meaning." Cousin Belle sighed. "You know, her mother— your grandmother—suffered this affliction as well. At first her doctors gave her opium, which only made matters worse, since it is addicting and for her brought on hallucinations. Then our family sent her to a special hospital for the mentally ill. Back then, in the twenties, their treatments were so . . . ill-informed . . . often more harmful than helpful . . . and frightening. She slipped farther away from us and finally into a pervasive delirium."

Cousin Belle paused, and I suddenly realized why she had insisted on installing our phone and that Mama call once a week. She drew in a deep, jangling breath before adding, "Your grandmother and I were best friends as well as cousins. There. I've just shared with you one of my greatest sorrows."

"I didn't know any of that," I murmured. "Did you?" I asked Katie.

"A little."

Cousin Belle reached out and patted my face.

"I have faith that someday medicine will be found that will help combat depression. Like that new penicillin they're talking about being an effective treatment for infections like pneumonia. Now that, child, would be quite the adventure. To be part of that discovery, wouldn't it?"

I frowned a bit. Yes, it would be, but . . .

Reading my doubt, Cousin Belle said, "Think because you're female, you can't make important discoveries in medicine?"

I hesitated.

"You do know about Madame Curie?"

Katie and I shook our heads.

"Good Lord. Why not?" Cousin Belle frowned. "Her work led to radiography, our being able to take X-rays of patients. She perfected it in World War I field hospitals. I met her once." She turned her head toward the direction of the library. "I believe I have a book about her." She waved her hand as if brushing off an errant thought.

"In the meantime," she continued, "until effective medicine is found, remember this: you can't fix your mama or save her on your own, as much as you want to. She has to fight her battles herself and to *want* to do so, to change—with our support, of course. Finding that resolve when lost in darkness is the hardest. What you can do to help is to show that you love her, that you want her to be well and strong, that you have faith in her ability to combat her demons, and then applaud her efforts and strength. Those things are all flares of light that she can push herself to follow. You can also help by once in a while bringing good cheer, giving her one of those 'somethings nice.' Things that are little joys in this world, that will coax her out from her own turmoil for a bit."

Cousin Belle held her hand out to me. "I think I have one—something that can give her a little sense of purpose, something that reaffirms life, as well as a bit of plain old amusement. Come. D'Artagnan has given birth to kittens! I wager that helping raise D'Artagnan's litter may be a bit of tonic for your mama . . . and for you."

CHAPTER 15

The next morning Cousin Belle loaded us into her bootlegger-fancy Ford and drove us home. Before we left, though, she'd fixed us an enormous breakfast of powdered-sugar waffles—Belgian, she'd called them. They melted in my mouth, I swear. While I was tasting something that sweet I could bear to talk on the something bitter—I'd told her about the check to Butler and asked what I should do about it.

"Your daddy handed you that?"

I nodded.

"And he asked that you give it to your mama?"

I nodded again.

Cousin Belle pressed her lips together and then stuck them out as if she were going to whistle and then pressed them closed again. Finally she said, "Let me think on that." I could tell she was smoldering about it, so I didn't push for more. She was still stewing on it as she drove along now—although I wasn't sure what aspect of that check was gnawing at her.

I was sitting in the back of the Ford on that creamy soft leather, steadying a laundry basket full of five kittens—striped, splotchy, black with white mittens—and D'Artagnan. Their eyes were still closed tight and their little heads wobbled as they clung close to their mama. I tried my best to keep their basket moored quietly with as little jostling as possible. When we did hit a bump and they bounced, their mews were like terrified bird chirps. D'Artagnan was purring to soothe them as best she could and licking them all over. She was a surprisingly tender mother for a cat named for a swashbuckling French soldier.

"We best give her a new name, hadn't we?" I asked.

"Why?" Cousin Belle called back to me.

"Because . . . well . . . because D'Artagnan is a boy name."

"Not necessarily," Cousin Belle replied. "All that name means is 'from Artagnan.'"

Cousin Belle turned onto our long drive, her wheels rumbling along the crushed oyster shells that served us as gravel. Up ahead, our white clapboard farmhouse came into view. I strained to see if the cotton eyelet curtains in Mama's bedroom were drawn tight, which would mean she was still abed—that she hadn't been able to summon up the will to face the day yet, that she was awash in . . . what was the word Cousin Belle had used? . . . *ennui.* I couldn't tell about the curtains, not yet. That's how long our driveway is, running along front fields used for corn and winter wheat. But I could see splashes of purple dancing along the house's face.

"Oh look," Katie said, "the lilacs are starting to bloom."

I squirmed forward to see for myself, immediately planning on cutting an armload to carry into Mama's bedroom. No person can resist the scent of life a lilac exudes with such joy in those cascades of tiny lavender-colored blossoms. Especially not a flower lover like Mama. That'd be two somethings nice I could bring her, I thought with a smile. Hopefully kittens and lilacs would overshadow my black eye and stitches and the dangerous moments that had brought them about—if I told the truth about the . . . the *encounter*, which I hadn't yet decided.

"Maybe I'll cut a few sprays to take back to the boarding house," Katie began, "they'd be a nice gift for—good grief!"

Cousin Belle slammed on the brakes. I had to quick throw myself over the basket to keep those kittens from flying while D'Artagnan set up a caterwaul of what for.

A big blur of mud and slop raced along the side of the car. I twisted to peer out the window. Oh God, it was our sow, Maizie, running at a clip that always stunned me when I saw her haul her baby-hippo self into a mad dash.

Oink-oink-oink-oink.

Five little blobs of dirty pink raced after her.

Instantly, Katie was out the door, calling, *Pig-pig-pig—hoooo—pig.*

A few seconds later Daddy rushed out of the woods, heaving, obviously lagging behind in the chase and winded as could be. He looked like he'd keel over any moment, his pneumonia-ravaged lungs fighting him.

"Doesn't that man know chasing a pig will only make it run faster?" murmured Cousin Belle, rolling down the window. "Russell!" she shouted. "Stop and catch your breath!"

But Daddy didn't hear. Or he ignored her and struggled on, wheezing hard.

"I know, I know," I said as Cousin Belle turned back toward me and started to speak. I was already moving to gently lift the basket of cats to be beside her so I could get out and help corral our pigs.

"Try to get him to stop," she said. "His getting

sick again isn't going to help matters, especially not for your mama. He won't listen to me. But he will you, child."

I had never asked before, but the question just popped out of me, given the to-the-bone-honest conversation we'd had the night before about Mama. "What's with it between you and Daddy? You don't like him, do you?"

Cocking her head and pushing her cat glasses back up her nose, Cousin Belle considered me a moment, blinking. "I wouldn't say that, child. I didn't like how your mama gave up her dreams to marry your daddy, no. And I certainly don't like the fact he gave you that check to deal with—that's not your job. But . . . I do like how he makes your mama laugh. And I very . . . very much like the fact that you exist." She reached out and gently tweaked my nose. "Now go help your daddy. I'll go on down to the house and check on your mama. But I won't show her the kittens. They'll be your gift."

I popped out of the car and darted into the woods, following the sound of Katie's calls. *Pig-pig-pig—hoooo—pig.*

I knew where Maizie was heading. We'd done this chase before. Every spring, in fact. That pig was after wild asparagus growing in the banks just across the back end of our creek.

"Daddy!" I called. I could hear him thrashing through underbrush ahead of me. "Daddy! Stop!" I finally caught up to him, bent over, his hands on his knees to hold himself up and coughing hard enough to spit up his lungs onto the ground.

When I reached him, his expression turned from pain to horror.

My hand shot up to my face. "It's not that bad, Daddy. Honest. I feel a lot better today."

"Damn it to hell, Lou!" He reached out and gathered me into his arms. He smelled of slime. He must have launched himself at our pigs and slid through muck and manure. "If something had happened to you, too . . ." He broke off and shook his head.

"But it didn't, Daddy." I tried to slough it off. "It was . . . a . . . a . . ." I couldn't think of what to call it, so I changed the subject. "You need to stop running, Daddy. You'll never catch Maizie chasing her. I know where she's heading and how to box her in."

Katie, Butler, and I had had to do this before, plenty, when Daddy and Will and Joe were off on their ships. Having spent so much of his life among waves and sea winds, Daddy must not remember farm ways, I realized. "Maizie must have dug herself under the fence, sensing that asparagus are growing on the creek banks. She can't resist them. She escapes like this every spring. She'll stop when she swims across the creek where it's narrowest and reaches those sprigs. Her piglets, too. They just follow her," I explained.

"But why is Katie calling then?" He pointed off in the distance, where Katie was still crooning *pig-pig-pig-hoooo-pig.*

"She's just making sure Maizie keeps heading that way and doesn't charge off to other pickings, where we can't corner her."

He looked at me blankly.

"Maizie's just like that. If she thinks you're calling her she's going to run the other way."

I braced myself for one of Daddy's goofy jokes about female fickleness. I know he's just teasing, but I don't always appreciate being poked at that way. I was surprised when all he grunted was *humph*.

"There is something that would really help, Daddy."

"What's that?"

"Butler used to—" I broke off. I needed Daddy to do what Butler had done when he, Katie, and I had had to pursue and hog-tie Maizie in the past. Which was to take our little skiff up the creek and safely beach it near where Maizie was rooting in the weeds. What stopped me short was I'd never before spoken of Butler in the past tense.

Butler.

I could hear Butler reciting a Lewis Carroll nonsense poem when we'd trailed Maizie last spring, about a pig at a pump wanting to jump:

> *By day and night he made his moan—*
> *It would have stirred a heart of stone*
> *to see him wring his hoofs and groan.*

I felt my eyes well up with tears. I wanted to kick myself. Was I going to get all weepy, all the time, at every single thought? I didn't have time for this right now—I needed to retrieve our stupid runaway pig.

Stare sorrow in the face. Recognize the pain for what it is. Cousin Belle whispered in my ear. *That takes honesty, courage, and a bit of spit. Which you have in spades, child.*

Mr. Cooper's voice came to me, too. *Those Brookes girls—pistols.*

So I tilted up my chin and stared into the startling, piercing anguish brought on all of a sudden by an everyday moment that should have passed with no big thought on it. Stood and let the tears about Butler fall, silent, waiting for them to stop so I could finish my thought about the skiff to Daddy.

Watching, Daddy's forehead furrowed with concern, then discomfort, and then he looked away from me. "Well, it sounds like you and Katie know what to do," he mumbled, turning to walk slowly back to the barn.

CHAPTER 16

Ever seen a pig swim? They're right good at it. And speedy as all get-out. No matter how gargantuan or how bitty they are. From the woods Katie was now calling to me. "Louisa! She's across already. Her piglets too. Get the skiff! Hurry!"

I hop-skipped myself into a sprint and raced to our dock. It's a long run, and by the time I'd gotten there I was as winded as Daddy. I scrambled down into our flat-bottom rowboat, leaning over a moment to catch my breath, fighting the nausea from the long dash. I am as good as any grown man in sculling, if I do say so myself. Butler had taught me well. But it requires strength, a steady hand, a clear head, and, for sure, a settled stomach. I took in deep breaths. C'mon, quit, I warned my body. Help me out here, even if my own father won't.

Lou-eeeeeee-saaa! Katie's call was distant now but pretty darn alarmed. Maizie must be showing signs of moving along to elsewhere.

I cupped my hand around my mouth and shouted as loud as I could along the water back to my sister. "COM-ING! HANG ON!"

Untying the skiff, I hauled up the thick oar, as long as I am tall. I slid it through the notch in the transom into the water. Holding it with both hands, I started sweeping the heavy oar's blade in a figure-eight swish to propel the boat forward. Fast.

There's a real trick to sculling with a single oar that most people have no idea how to do. For children of the Tidewater, though, it's second nature, like walking. It's the way we can traverse the narrow channels of our marshes—regular rowing oars need a wide berth and get stuck in the shallows. We stand while we twist the single pole oar with both hands, using our entire bodies rather than just one arm. On our feet, we can also see over the reeds and not get lost in the marshy labyrinth. Trust me, once you've been swallowed up in cattails and cord grass in a dead-end turn, you never want to repeat that experience of being marooned in mud and mosquitoes, completely hidden from help.

I pushed to the right with my left hand and then immediately to the left with my right, flicking my wrists, over and under, in a tight, constant serpentine motion.

Normally, I loved the dip and sway of the boat reacting to the fishtail-like twist of the oar. To keep moving forward, when I push the oar to the right, I need to shift my weight to my left foot, and then switch to my right foot when I push left. A shimmy dance along the water, in silent symbiosis with the currents, that lets me get up close to gliding muskrats and ducks as if I were one of them, a thing of the natural world.

But now I just needed to move as quickly as possible.

Louuuuu—eeeeeeee—sa!

I swiveled the oar faster.

Within a few moments, I was passing the edges of Emmett's place, vaguely aware that he'd come out of their cottage and was shadowing me, running alongside the water, shouting encouragement. Then I rounded the bend to see Katie ahead, up to her knees on one side of the creek, Maizie and her brood on the other. The pigs were rooting and grunting so happy and loud, I could hear them from my distance. I could even spot the clods of dirt they were knocking up into the air with their snouts as they gorged on asparagus stems.

I stopped in mid-scull. *Oh no.* In my haste, I'd forgotten rope to hog-tie Maizie. Well, I could use the boat's line for that. But I'd also forgotten a pail of food to coerce her. I wanted to kick myself.

There's a reason chasing a greased pig is sport at county fairs. It's near impossible to nab one once they are all wet and glistening, as Maizie and her piggies would be from their swim. She'd need persuasion, not pursuit. Only then could we truss her to the skiff and get her to swim back to the farm.

Should I go back? I glanced over my shoulder and saw Emmett trotting along the bank to catch up to me.

"Hey LJ, glad to see you finally took my advice!" Emmett called.

"What are you talking about?"

"Letting the hog loose to flush out your mama."

I bit my tongue from noting once again what a dumb-bunny idea that was. "It was an accident!" I called. Then I realized he could save me. "Hey, Emmett?"

"Yeah?"

"I need your help. Can you get me some scraps to entice Maizie? A little something. Please?" I knew that was a big ask of Emmett. Nothing was spared in that lean household of his. But he darted back to his cottage to retrieve what he could.

I sculled on to pull alongside Katie.

"Where's Daddy?" she asked, as she rolled herself into the skiff while I listed myself to the other side against her motion. We both rotated inward at the same time to keep the boat from flipping.

"He went back to the house," I answered, picking up the oar again.

Katie scowled but said nothing.

I turned the skiff back toward Emmett's place, where I could see him coming with a bucket and trailing siblings. "This little piggy went to market. This little piggy stayed home," they chanted.

I fluttered the oar to wiggle the boat into shore for Emmett to hand me a pail of fish-heads and tails. The stench about knocked me into the water.

"Sorry." He shrugged. "That's what Granny had."

"Oh Lord." Katie gagged. "Let's be quick about it."

Maizie, however, had other ideas.

I got us onto the opposite bank and before we could offer her the fish pail, Maizie bolted up its slope. Katie plunged out of the skiff and scrambled after her. Maizie dashed back down, sliding almost within reach of me. Katie tumbled along behind.

Oink-oink-oink-oink, her piglets chorused, racing around in circles.

Maizie took off along the shoreline, flattening all vegetation like a giant rolling pin. Katie stumbled behind—falling, getting up, falling, and getting up.

"Hell's bells," she shouted in frustration.

Oink-oink-oink-oink.

I quickly tied a slipknot in my boat's rope and waited, crouched, ready. The stinky pail in one hand, the noose in another, I prayed Katie would manage to get ahead of Maizie and turn her around and back toward me.

Another grunting-scurrying up the embankment, another tumbling down—the hog and my sister in a blur of mud and brush.

Oink-oink-oink-oink.

Rolling into the water's edge, Kate got to her knees and launched herself at Maizie, actually catching the pig's big fat rear end. But Maizie popped free like a squeezed bar of soap and barreled forward, lunging toward me.

Oink-oink-oink-oink.

When she was about three gallop-steps from me, I hurled those fish parts in a cloud of stench onto the mud.

I swear that sow did as sudden and crazy-eyed a full stop as the Looney Tunes' cartoon Porky Pig. I could almost hear the movie sound effects of her putting on her proverbial brakes: *eeeeerrrrrrrk-kkkkk.*

She started gobbling.

"Quick!" Katie urged, her hand and knees still in the mud.

Butler would have been proud. Just as I had witnessed his doing repeatedly, I got the noose around Maizie's log-thick neck and cinched in no time flat.

"YAAAYYY!" Emmett's little sisters and brothers cheered from down the creek.

After my mud-pie of a sister managed to get herself out of the muck and crawled into the boat, we hitched Maizie to us and pushed off. She swam beside the skiff, clearly thoroughly pleased with herself. Her children splashed along behind. I kept close to our side of the creek in case the piglets needed a moment on shore to rest. But they floated along easily. The tide was with us going home.

"Bacon, bacon, we love bacon," Emmett's family chanted until he shooed them away, embarrassed by their obvious campaign for payback come hog-killing season.

It only took about seven minutes, I'd say, to be within view of our dock. That's when I did a cartoon-worthy double-take myself.

Daddy was waiting for us at the pier with a hammer to repair the fencing once we'd gotten our pigs back into their pen. But that's not what startled me and sent my heart contorting with a little spasm of hope. Only a few yards away from Daddy stood Mama, leaning on Cousin Belle!

Mama was up and out of that bedroom where she'd been languishing so long? Because of a pig hunt?

Granny would say that what your mama needs is a good jolt to get her going again. Like a tractor that's been sitting idle and rusting.

If Emmett's corncob-pipe-smoking, crab-picking, knife-wielding granny turned out to be right—that something silly like our hog getting loose could resuscitate Mama, no matter how momentarily—I might just want to kiss that crazy boy, I thought with some astonishment.

The biggest miracle, though, was not just that Mama was standing outside, where the sweet-smelling fresh air might blow away some of her pain and fill her with spring, but that she was within talking distance of Daddy. I could tell they weren't conversing or anything, but that was the first time my parents had been in view of one another for weeks—ever since that horrible night Mama's misery got the better of her and she let fly what her tortured, grieving soul believed—that Daddy had killed Butler by talking him into helping out on that ill-fated voyage. For books and date money.

Maybe? Oh please, maybe. Could it be true? Could forgiveness be in bloom on that dock? I felt Katie suck in her breath, sudden and sharp, as a shiver of optimism ran through her as well.

But my heart sank back down just as quickly as it had rejoiced. That check. That official notification from the coast guard. I remembered how Daddy's face had crumpled as he held those papers in his hands, by the barn in that twilight. It was the same devastated expression he had the night Mama lost herself to despair and accusation. I had seen Daddy taking baby steps toward recovery from that awful scene before those two envelopes arrived. Now, on our pier, he was still slumped and mournful-looking—nothing like my daddy of the before.

What would Mama do if she knew the navy had officially determined that Daddy's phone call home to reassure her they were safe out on the waters had been the very beacon that led the Nazis straight to Butler? Would she blame herself, her nervousness, for her baby boy's death? Lord knows the local gossips would.

I was learning that blame was like the sea nettles that clog the bay in the summer, their threads of poison floating outstretched, waiting. The first brush of one of those long tentacles would sting a little—survivable, for sure, but definitely enough to slow a thing down. The kill came when that jellyfish quick-closed its fanned-out strings to entangle the injured prey, the repeated burns rendering the victim incapable of swimming away and saving itself.

The question—*what if*—was the first sting that began the death-dance of blame. Then followed the self-flogging: What if Daddy's regular seaman hadn't gotten sick? What if Daddy hadn't asked Butler to stand in for the guy? What if Butler hadn't felt guilty about the impending cost of his books for college? What if Daddy had listened to Mama's fears? What if Mama had more of that "quiet mind" Mrs. Roosevelt talked about? What if Daddy hadn't called home that night?

On the dock, Mama started clapping as she spotted our ridiculous little flotilla of boat and pigs. Clapping with delight as she sometimes did with the little jokes I told her.

"Oh, praise God, look at her," Katie murmured. She started waving to Mama.

Mama let go of Cousin Belle to stand on her toes and wave back in happy sweeps of her arms.

Watching Katie and Mama's amusement I kept sculling, but I felt myself flush with a grin as big as Maizie. And I swore to myself right then that I'd never share with Mama what Daddy had told me was in that letter. It'd kill the glimmer of rebirth I was seeing in her at that moment. Maybe altogether, maybe for forever.

I got us to the dock.

"Katydid, sweetheart," Mama sang out. "Oh my goodness. Look at you!" She laughed that wonderful, sunny little peal of mirth of hers, when she could see up close how lathered with creek-bank slime poor Katie was.

Then she caught sight of me—my bruises and stitches.

And she fainted.

CHAPTER 17

When Mama came to, her head propped up on Cousin Belle's lap, I wasn't about to tell her the absolute truth about my bruises and stitches. That I had banged my head, for sure, but not that it had happened because of some green air corps cadets hopped up to hunt Nazis. Besides being worried sick, she'd never let me out in a boat again.

Don't tell Mama was as much a credo among my brothers and sister as *find her a somethings nice.* All my life I'd been warned against upsetting

Mama by telling things she didn't *have* to know, things that might knock her into one of her fogs of anxiety.

Like the time Katie got into a brawl in the schoolyard with a stuck-up chit of a girl who was making fun of a child who came to school barefoot until the first frost in order to save wear-and-tear on her one pair of shoes. (That was tough to hide since it was our preacher's daughter that did the teasing.) Or Joe having to clean blackboard erasers for a month after school on account of putting a bullfrog in his algebra teacher's desk—which he told Katie he'd done because he had a crush on the young woman and wanted to dispel that nonsense in his head right quick. Or my not explaining that the cast I had on my arm for a month came about because Emmett had convinced me I could safely do a Peter Pan off the hayloft into a new high-mound of cut hay. (I don't know why I listen to that boy.)

And then, of course, the very last time—when Butler and I had hidden that empty life jacket we'd found floating, all charred and mangled, and not told Mama.

So the fib rolled out of me as inevitable as breakers on a beach. I have to say, though, there's a new weight on my heart each and every time I've had to hide something from my mama for fear of upsetting her. And this one also hurt my pride considerably. "Oh, Mama, it was the stupidest thing," I said. "I wasn't paying enough attention. I was all distracted when I spotted an osprey, it was that beautiful—and I managed to run the boat aground. With a big ole jolt. And . . . and I fell into the wheel. You know how you and Daddy always say"—I glanced up at him, standing a few feet back, hopeful that including him might make her look at him or him step closer—"that I have such a hard head? Well, I guess you're right—no give there to prevent it splitting open on impact. We're lucky it didn't destroy the wheel." I forced a little laugh.

Daddy walked away, muttered about seeing to the hogs.

Katie's eyes welled with tears watching him go. After a moment, she got up off the ground where she was kneeling beside Mama to help him. I realized how hard it must be for my sister, coming and going from the shipyard. Each time she came home meant seeing things afresh. When you sit in things all the time you get more used to them.

I kept my voice breezy. "The doctor said the scar will hardly show once it's healed, Mama."

Stroking Mama's head soothingly, Cousin Belle chimed in. "That's right, Ruth. He'll pull the stitches out in seven days. I'll come get Louisa June and take her to his office. He did a fine job, as good as any plastic surgeon might." She looked up from Mama's face into mine to catch my gaze and make sure I was absorbing what she was saying so we kept our story straight between us. "That's why Russell called me to get Louisa June. He knew the Hampton doctors might be a little more experienced with careful stitching."

"Russell called you?" Mama looked up at Cousin Belle with a pleased look of surprise.

"Wonders of wonders." Cousin Belle smiled down at her. I marveled at Cousin Belle's quick fiction that fed Mama something she'd like to hear. Then I worried if Cousin Belle had ever worked me in that way. I'd hate to not be able to trust what she told me—that wonderful old eccentric was becoming mighty important to me.

Mama turned to me. "The ospreys are back?"

"Yes, ma'am."

Mama reached up and touched my cheek. "Your poor face," she murmured.

"It's no big deal, Mama." I made myself grin. "It's not like it's Katie's."

"No." She nodded, talking more to herself than to me.

Even though I'd made the joke, her reply did sting a bit, I must admit.

e◡∂

It took a boatload of coaxing, but Cousin Belle convinced Mama to stay downstairs in the kitchen while Katie made lunch. Talk about wonders of wonders—it was the first time Mama had been in that room since Butler's death. Cousin Belle can be awful persuasive. It helped a little that none of us had ever claimed a regular chair for meals. We'd shifted around, since our family grew and shrank regularly depending on when Daddy, Will, and Joe shipped out, so there wasn't one specific to Butler. But it still was hard being around our table without his smile and verse.

As soon as she sat down, Mama got jittery. So Cousin Belle sent me out for that "just-because present you brought home." I was out and back with that basket of kittens quick—with D'Artagnan caterwauling at me for jostling them again.

"Oh, ooh, look," Mama crooned, gently cupping the faces of each of those tiny felines. "They're just darling. Ohhh."

D'Artagnan purred up a storm, as if she understood exactly what Mama had said about her babies and was bursting with pride. "June-Bug," Mama said, "fetch a saucer of milk for the mother, won't you? She's got to keep up her strength."

"I'm telling you," Cousin Belle whispered at me. "Cats. Every time."

Indeed, there was something magical about that moment. With the basket of cats by her side, Mama even ate all her lunch, including the canned green beans from last August's crop. I can't stand that particular vegetable myself. Maybe because seeing them brings on the memory of the week-long ache in my back from leaning over to pick those knee-high bushes, row after row, in scorching Tidewater heat.

Noticing me pushing beans around on my plate—the fact she was attuned to things around her was another hopeful sign—Mama reached over with her fork to shove a few toward me. "Eat up, honey, you need the vitamins to heal." She watched me swallow, fighting a gag. "You sure you're feeling all right?"

I nodded, smiling.

A cloud drifted onto her face. "You got all those bruises from the wheel?"

She glanced at Cousin Belle and then at Katie. "Really?"

"Want some tea, Mama?" Katie jumped up and went for the teakettle.

"Noooo, thank you, Katydid." Mama's eyes came back to me.

I made myself eat another bean, concentrating on my plate, avoiding her gaze. Mama's surfacing made me want to shout hallelujahs, but I also knew that while I fibbed pretty easily to hide alarming things from her, I usually had a hard time sticking to those tales if she was well enough to scrutinize.

"I would love some tea, Katie," Cousin Belle announced, keeping Katie at the stove, away from Mama's questions. "Do tell about Newport News and the shipyard while the water boils. Anytime I head that way I'm absolutely shocked by the traffic. I swear Newport News, Hampton Roads, and Norfolk have doubled in population with all these wartime workers."

"You should try riding the trolley," Katie answered. "Sometimes we have to hang on from the outside, so many bodies are crammed into the car and spilling out its edges. Unless, of course, there are newbie sailors on it—they are more than willing to give up their seats for a smile."

"Oh dear," Mama murmured.

"Don't worry, Mama." Katie laughed. "It's mostly harmless gallantry. Those boys are trying so hard to seem grown up and brave. There's a real sense of camaraderie on the streets. A sense of pulling together—men and women, old and young. Especially around the shipyard. It runs round the clock, you know, in shifts. Herds of us come in at pretty much the same time another mass of workers is leaving. There's a lot of calling back and forth. 'Sleep tight,' or 'have a good day,' or good-natured ribbing like, 'don't be messing up my good work.' That kind of thing. The ships are built from the bottom up, so whatever one shift has just finished working on, the next continues. So there's some competitive banter thrown around."

"Is it hard work, honey?"

Katie and I exchanged a look, and I knew my sister was thinking about Emma and her hurt eyes. "It can be, Mama," she answered carefully. "But I really do enjoy it. It's . . . really . . . satisfying. I feel good knowing I'm helping our country. And honestly, it's like sewing. I'm just putting together two pieces of metal instead of fabric, and a good weld actually makes a beautiful pattern, Mama. I have to be careful, though, the thing that sticks those sheets of metal together has to be stronger than either of them—and that's me, my weld, my hand-iwork. Can't be any bubbles, or it'll break apart. I work down in the double bottoms, in two-foot squares that hold the ballast and keep the boat upright in high seas." She paused. "And I'm good at it, Mama. Really good. Even the most contrarian supervisor says so. Proud of me?"

Proud of me, Mama? Hearing my big sister ask the question that always roiled inside me was one of those clearing-cloud moments, when sun breaks through a haze and lights up truth. *Proud of me, Mama?* That was the ultimate somethings nice, wasn't it? Or at least that's what my siblings and I hoped—that we mattered to her that much, that giving her something to be proud of gave her a beacon she could follow to lift herself out of darkness, like Cousin Belle had said to Katie and me at her kitchen table.

I suddenly heard Joe's voice asking Mama that very question the last night we were all together.

I suspect Mama had that flash of memory about Joe, too, because her voice was hoarse when she answered, "Always, sugar, always."

Right then, I swear that very moment, the phone rang. Just as I was thinking on Joe. My blood ran cold. What if I had tempted fate somehow?

I looked to Mama. All the color had drained from her face. I wanted to reach out and take her hand, maybe get a little reassuring squeeze from a parent and give one in return. But I was frozen solid in my chair. And Mama was as still and pale as a statue. I guess we'd always be afraid when that phone rang now.

Katie answered it. She hadn't been home the night Daddy called, the night the Nazis hunted Butler down. So the telephone ringing wouldn't paralyze her. She could still move.

"Hey, Mrs. McGrath. . . . Yes, ma'am. Doing all right." Katie rolled her eyes in an impatient expression of *get on with it, lady.* She listened for a few more seconds to our local party line operator, the bearer of news, good and bad, happy and devastating. "Yes, ma'am. . . . Yes . . . I'll tell her you asked after her. . . . Is there someone on the line for us, Mrs. McGrath?"

I'm not sure I breathed, waiting.

"Hey!" Katie lit up. "Where are you?" She waved at Mama to come to the phone.

Mama didn't budge, still ghostly white.

Katie beckoned harder. "Mama, it's Joe!"

Mama shook her head. I knew what she was afraid of—that if she took that call it might be the last time she heard his voice, too.

Covering the receiver, Katie said more urgently, "Mama, he's asking for you. He only has a minute."

Mama shook her head.

"Ruth." Cousin Belle stood and took Mama by the elbow. "Get up now, honey. Your son needs you." She pulled Mama to her feet.

"Joe," Mama murmured and then rushed forward, taking the phone from Katie.

"Should I get Daddy?" I whispered.

"No time. He's about to board a troop train."

"Florida?" Mama listened for a moment. "I love you, honey. Be safe." She let her forehead fall to the wall beside the phone. "Be safe. Be safe. Be safe."

Gently, Katie took the receiver from Mama's hand and hung it up. "If he's going to Florida, Mama, I bet they're sending him to a special school at Key West. We've heard at the shipyard that the navy has a new technology that can detect submarines underwater. Like throwing radio beams into the depths and listening for it to bump up against objects. That's . . . only the best of the best are trusted with doing that, Mama. The navy must be really impressed with Joe."

Mama managed a nod as she backed herself away from the wall and turned toward the stairs, silent, pale, that unnerving soothsayer look on her face. But she did gather up the basket of kittens and D'Artagnan to take with her.

CHAPTER 18

When Cousin Belle returned me home from the doctor's appointment—my forehead no longer looking like Frankenstein's, sprouting black thread—she'd gone to the barn to talk with Daddy. I watched through the kitchen window as she called to him and he ventured out—reluctantly. After a moment they headed for the dock, I suspect because Mama's room didn't have a view out that way.

At first, in reaction to whatever Cousin Belle was saying to him, Daddy looked like he was throwing all kinds of attitude at her. His dislike, or defiance, or discomfort with her had straightened his spine in a way I hadn't seen for a long time. I must admit the sight irritated me some, seeing that orneriness would energize him while other things didn't. His walking away from me during the Maizie escapade still stung.

Daddy paced along the length of our deadrise— which had been returned to our pier, bright with new paint—his hands clasped behind his back as I'd always imaged his doing along the deck of his tugboat. Occasionally, he'd gesture dismissively at her. But Cousin Belle persisted in whatever she was saying, standing just as erect, just as commanding as he was. Eventually his stride slowed to a stop. He clearly was listening. Then he bowed slightly and withdrew to his barnyard sanctuary. Whatever point Cousin Belle had argued, she'd won.

She came inside and found me in the kitchen. "I was speaking to your daddy about that check he burdened you . . ." She stopped abruptly and began again. "I spoke to him about the check to Butler that he . . . entrusted . . . to you. I am going to take you to the bank in Hampton, where I have my accounts. I'll help you deposit it there."

Cousin Belle sat down by the table and patted the chair beside her. I nestled into it. "Your daddy and I have agreed that Butler would want you to have that money, to start a little nest egg for your own education."

I frowned. "I . . . I don't want it, Cousin Belle. That money is . . ." I trailed off. How could I explain that the check felt like the worst kind of blood money? "It belongs to Butler. He earned it."

"Child," she said gently, and took my hand, waiting, not stating the obvious that my dead brother couldn't spend his twenty-three dollars and twenty-five cents.

I bit my lip.

"You are a smarty-pants in the best possible way, Louisa June." Cousin Belle squeezed my hand. "Don't you think you deserve to go to college, just like Butler was planning to?"

I honestly had never thought about it before. Did I want to live up to my name to please my book-loving Mama? Sure. Had I wanted to be well read so I could have things to talk to Butler about? Yes. But I'd never really thought through the end-game of that—of actually *going* to college myself someday. I shrugged.

"Don't sell yourself short, child." She patted my hand. "Butler wouldn't like it."

I sucked in my breath, startled by her words.

Cousin Belle stood. "Let's wait two weeks for all those bruises to completely fade so you don't have to be bothered with explaining them to strangers. And wear a Sunday dress, child. After visiting the bank, I'll treat us to lunch and an afternoon at the Chamberlin-Vanderbilt Hotel."

Two weeks later, I sat on our wraparound porch, waiting for Cousin Belle. It was now June, and the air was sweet with the scent of the saucer-sized magnolia blossoms on the tree in front of our house. Basking like one of Cousin Belle's cats in the warm sunshine, I tugged a little at the dress I'd borrowed from Katie's things. I'd shot up in height since last spring, and my own three dresses were suddenly way too short for a fancy place like the Chamberlin-Vanderbilt. So I'd picked one of Katie's prettiest—a blue-and-white seersucker, with a suit-like collar, belted at the waist, and neat stitched-down pleats in the skirt.

I didn't exactly fill its blouse, but a few quick tucks had fixed that. I'd even managed to do my long hair up in what Mama's *Ladies Home Journal* magazine called a coronet. I'd parted it down the middle and made two long braids that I then wrapped over the top of my head and pinned at the nape of my neck. I couldn't do anything about my childhood bangs—even though no teenage girl wanted those anymore and swept them up off her face—because I needed them to cover up my scar. The gash was definitely beginning to fade but right then was still red and angry-looking.

"My goodness, you look lovely, June-Bug," Mama had said when I went into her room to say goodbye. She was actually sitting up in her bed, surrounded by crawling kittens. She even held a book in her hand as if she were considering reading it. I checked the title—*Wuthering Heights*. I'd need to find a way to swap that out with some-thing a little less haunted without her noticing. That collection of Dorothy Parker, maybe. I didn't get all the author's jabs at grown-up shenanigans, but I could tell if I did I'd laugh—which would be good for a little wake up of laughter for Mama.

"Tell me all about the Chamberlin when you get home?" she asked, interrupting my thoughts.

"I promise, Mama. Every little detail."

She smiled. "It was the premier resort of the East Coast once upon a time. . . . Very F. Scott Fitzgerald–like . . . orchestras . . . evening attire . . . Originally built by a Mississippi riverboat gambler, you know." She shifted on her pillows, and her voice grew stronger. "We used to go there every Sunday when I was little. It was such a treat. The chef had come down from New York City, and his desserts were heavenly. Oh my, I can still taste that delicious German chocolate cake, he—" She broke off. "I . . . I don't suppose they make that anymore." Her gaze and her thoughts drifted out the window.

I sighed. There she went. Because of cake. No thought seemed safe these days with her.

Suddenly, D'Artagnan returned from a prowl and catapulted from the floor onto Mama's lap and circled five or six times before settling down atop her legs. Mama reached down to stroke the cat's head—for that moment tethered again.

Maybe I'd be able to reel Mama back in to me pretty easily when I came home—if I had some good stories of my day's experiences. I vowed to rake in a bucket of them.

⌒⌒

Not at the bank, of course. That visit had to remain secret. But I longed to describe to Mama how all those bow-tied men sitting at desks jumped to their feet and yanked on their lapels to straighten their jackets when Cousin Belle walked through the door. One poor fellow was so discombobulated that when he bolted out of his wooden seat so fast, it fell to the polished floor with an echoing crash. All his colleagues froze, like they'd been caught passing notes in class. I didn't know fifty-year-old men could turn as ruby red as an embarrassed teenager.

No one moved until Cousin Belle waved regally at them, saying, "Please, gentlemen, please don't let me interrupt your work."

While they glanced around, no man wanting to be the first to sit back down, a secretary hurried forward. "Miss Archer, how lovely to see you today. Mr. Williams is expecting you."

"Good morning, Gertrude. Let me introduce my young cousin, Louisa June Brookes."

The lady shook my hand and then led us toward a spiral staircase, spinning upward in front of an ornate gilded cage that protected a train-car-size safe. The bank building was one enormous, vaulting, two-story room, crowned by a wide balcony where sat its bespectacled president, overlooking the floor below like Zeus from a cloudbank. Even wreathed in the dignity and authority of his office, Mr. Williams rose quickly as Cousin Belle approached. She put her arm around my shoulders protectively. "Harold," she said—I could tell that no one else dared use that gentleman's first name—"I bring you your newest depositor."

I pulled Butler's check from my wallet, still crumpled from my fury the night Daddy handed it to me. I smoothed it out as best I could on Mr. Williams's boat-size desk. He had all the necessary paperwork prepared already—including a transfer of one hundred, seventy-six dollars and seventy-five cents from Cousin Belle's checking account!

My mouth dropped open.

"Don't want to catch flies, child," Cousin Belle whispered at me, patting my hand.

"But, Cousin Belle, that's . . . that's . . ."

"A deposit combined with your check that totals two hundred dollars—the equivalent of a year's in-state tuition for William & Mary, I believe," Mr. Williams said. "Sign here, Miss Brookes." He unscrewed the top of a golden fountain pen and handed it to me. Of course, I made a big ink splotch as I scratched out my name, too stunned to think straight. But he just blew on the ink to dry it, then recorded my first deposit on the ledger, stamped it, and handed me the little black account book—a pocket-size tablet that completely changed the possibilities of my life.

I turned to Cousin Belle, speechless.

"That's Butler's legacy." She smiled at me reassuringly. "That's what he would want. I am certain of it. Your daddy too. Of course, you have to study very hard to be accepted." She rose and held her hand out for mine. "Time for lunch. Shall we?"

At the palatial Chamberlin-Vanderbilt Hotel, the white-jacketed maître d' ushered us to one of the very best tables on the veranda, overlooking the resort's sandy beach. Built beside Fort Monroe on Old Point Comfort—the last little spit of land that wades out into the Chesapeake Bay—the hotel blessed me with an uninterrupted view of blue sky and blue water, all the way to where the bay and the ocean meet in a rough-and-tumble embrace—some thirty miles in the distance.

I drank in the gentle breeze and filled myself with peacefulness. The waves in front of us were mere ripples, tranquil and sparkling, like what I thought heaven might be like if it were watery. I shaded my eyes to gaze out and out and out.

"Sorry for the fracas, Miss Archer," our waiter apologized as he put down appetizers of iced shrimp on the white linen tablecloth with way too much silverware for anybody to know how to make good use of.

Cousin Belle tapped a miniature fork with long prongs laid perpendicularly across my setting. I picked it up and dug into my first fat shrimp as she said, "I had wondered what all that banging was, Walter."

"We've been ordered to take down the hotel's two cupolas. They can be seen out on the ocean, way beyond Cape Henry. Isn't that the darndest thing?" He lowered his voice and added, "They're worried a German warship cruising offshore could use the spires as sightlines to target Fort Monroe."

"German battleships?" I asked. "Battleships? Not just U-boats?"

"Yes, miss. Preparing for possibilities. Although those gentlemen"—he nodded at some naval officers sitting two tables away from us—"would tell you there aren't any U-boats round here." He winked at me before leaving us to our meal.

When it came time to order dessert, Walter shared more information the navy lieutenant commanders would probably prefer he not. It started with his saying, "I have one snowball left. Would you like to order it?"

"What's a snowball?" I asked.

"Oh, it's one of the most delectable concoctions you'll ever have," Cousin Belle said. "A generous scoop of the richest vanilla ice cream I've ever tasted, made here by the chef, rolled in fresh coconut, and topped with chocolate ganache." She looked up at Walter. "Only one?"

"Yes, ma'am, I'm sorry. This morning we used the last bit of our vanilla bean and coconut. We keep hoping for a new shipment to come, but merchant ships seem to keep getting . . ." He paused and looked meaningfully at the officers. "Lost . . . somewhere south of here. And of course, most boats now are carrying machine parts and whatnot. No dessert ingredients. Sugar will be the next to go."

"Then do bring us that snowball, please, Walter. Quick! Before someone steals it!" Cousin Belle said.

"Oh, don't worry yourself, Miss Archer. I told the kitchen I was asking you if you wanted it. No one will touch it before I get back." He grinned. "If they know what's good for them."

We shared it. Cousin Belle was right—it was de-li-cious—maybe even more so knowing that the sumptuous dessert might be the last of its kind for quite a while.

ℰ—∂

After such a feast, I fairly waddled out to the beach. I flopped into one of the brightly colored canvas hammock chairs lined up in neat rows along the water's edge. At home, I'd discovered that I'd outgrown my bathing suit as well, so I'd brought short culottes and a cotton shirt to change into. I was a little self-conscious, looking around at all the women in their Hollywood-glamour suits, with matching robes and wide sunhats, knowing I looked pretty darn bumpkin and out of place.

Of course, that was nothing when compared to Cousin Belle's getup. She emerged from the changing rooms in a swimming *dress*, with a sailor collar—like the ones you see on Victorian postcards. All conversation around me stopped as the sunbathers watched her cross the sands to me. Noticing my gape, Cousin Belle straightened her cat glasses and asked, "Do you think you'd prefer seeing this old body in a two-piece?"

"N-n-no, ma'am," I murmured, hoping that was the right answer.

"Here's my philosophy, child, if I'm not comfortable wearing something, I'm not going to, no matter how many people around me do." She opened her bag and pulled out several books. She handed me Louisa May Alcott's *Eight Cousins*. "You'll enjoy this. A girl finding her way with old aunties and cousins after her father dies."

She opened her own book, *The Age of Innocence*.

"Who wrote that?" I asked, trying to ignore the sniggers of people around us.

"Edith Wharton. She won a Pulitzer for it—the very first woman to be honored with that prize. She wrote all manner of things. Including reports from Europe during the war."

"Don't tell me. You met her in France, right?"

Cousin Belle smiled. "I did. A brilliant thinker." She began reading.

I opened my book and began chuckling pretty much right away. Alcott's portraits of people were so amusing. After an hour or so, I stole a glance at Cousin Belle in her antiquated bathing garb and her sparkly cat glasses and wondered how the novelist might describe her—with affection? Satire? Admiration?

I turned my gaze forward, to the golden tinge spreading along the waves in the now late-afternoon light. I hardly ever just sit by the water and enjoy it. Even on our dock, I usually have a long pole net with me, on watch for crabs exploring the edges of our pilings. With their pinchers sapphire-blue and tipped in red, they are easy to spot in still shallows. None of my family wastes time simply idling when we might could pull up dinner.

Here, though, I didn't have to do that. I found my eyes lifted to the horizon and the seemingly endless expanse of blue disappearing into clouds and journeys to the beyond. On the other end of all those waves—three thousand miles of them— lay France. The land of adventures—for Cousin Belle anyway. I let my mind wander over the idea of traveling there someday, like she had, then on the new, breathtaking idea of my going to college. For a moment, the war, my grief, slept quiet and left me alone. I was free. I imagined adventures. Of my own making.

A few tugs and pilot boats began filling the vista heading out to sea. Then, around the corner of Cape Henry, a sliver of gray appeared. Then another. And another. Single file. Getting bigger, heading my way. A convoy of merchant ships coming in. Maybe one of them was bringing in more vanilla bean and coconut.

I was just starting to nudge Cousin Belle to say so, when the sands quaked underneath me.

An enormous volcano of spray erupted out on the horizon, followed by flames and black smoke billowing up and up, and then the bone-shaking sound *KABOOM* caught up, rattling the hotel's windows behind us. I pole-vaulted to my feet as people around me shrieked.

One of those ships was burning, sinking fast, bow first.

CHAPTER 19

"We're under attack!" "Look! Look there!" "That ship's on fire!" "Was it torpedoed?"

Ever seen a squabble of gulls get surprised, how they take off in a jumble of fear and noise, bashing into each other and squawking?

Most of those glamour-girl women fled, squealing, leaving behind their magazines, their sandals, their sun lotion, their straw bags. They bumped into men rushing toward the water, cursing, jostling each other to get a better look.

Slowly, Cousin Belle rose. She stood her ground, taking my elbow. "Stay close by me, Louisa."

I barely heard her. My heart was pounding. *So that's what it looked like. A ship hit, in flames, going down. The last image Butler would have seen of this world as he was thrown into the Atlantic to die. Oh, Butler.*

Inky smoke from the exploded tanker bloated and thickened as quick and terrifying as a hurricane squall line. Within a few moments, I could no longer see if the ship was above water, it was so engulfed. *Where were the sailors in that inferno? The old men like Mr. Cooper. The husbands and fathers like my daddy. The boys. The brothers. Butler.*

The chatter around me grew feverish with anxiety. "Sweet Jesus, what did that?" "Was it the Nazis?" "Where the hell is our navy?"

From behind us came a whine and buzz, surging louder and louder. Planes.

The people on the beach pivoted, a few ducking under beach umbrellas, as if that would protect them against bombs falling from the sky.

I couldn't make myself turn to look up to make sure they weren't the Luftwaffe descending upon us from God knows where, just like the Japanese Zeros had suddenly materialized over Pearl Harbor and laid waste to all on the ground below them. I was transfixed on the horizon and its desperate scene. *That's what it had looked like.*

"Planes," Cousin Belle said. "Ours."

Varoom. Varoom. Varoom. Varoom.

A squadron of small army bombers, just like the ones that had nearly done in Emmett and me, hurtled over us, heading out to sea, clearly on a real U-boat hunt this time.

People around us cheered. "Go get 'em, boys!"

I kept my eyes on those airplanes until they reached the horizon, where sea and sky met, where a ship had turned into a hell on earth. The planes circled. I wondered how much fuel they had. They circled and circled. Could those flames scorch the pilots' eyes, like those welding torches had Emma's?

Ten minutes passed as those planes circled. Smoke raged on, swelling up into a fiendish, swirling apocalypse.

To the south of us, from the direction of the Norfolk Naval Base, an observation blimp drifted into view and started to lumber out over the waters. A little fleet of coast guard surfboats zipped past the Chamberlin's beachfront. Yachts with their sails unfurling as they hurriedly put out to sea followed them. Suddenly the bay was swarming with fireboats and navy cutters and small rescue boats on their way to the convoy.

More cheers from the crowd that was growing larger by the second. Now that they could see those boats providing cover for them, more spectators sauntered out, bringing their veranda cocktails as if they were gathering to watch a Kentucky Derby horse race. It took every sermon and Alcott story I'd read preaching tolerance to not jump them and shove their faces into the sand.

Most around us, however, were horrified. They were frozen, hands to their throats or mouths. Did they feel as useless and helpless as I did? As forever changed by the sight?

That's what it had looked like. Oh, Butler.

Out on the burning horizon, the convoy's other

freighters and tankers were scattering from the roaring flames of the dying ship, trying to reach port as quickly as possible on their own. Breaking up the convoy's single-file line meant giving up the protection of its escort destroyer. She was sure to be World War I vintage, but that was better than nothing. I imagined the panic onboard those behemoth ships, slowed and clumsy by the weight of oil and cargo in the bellies. So close to having survived their voyage, now in such danger within view of safe harbor. So slow. Easy pickings.

Oh God, help them hurry. Hurry.

"What the hell are they doing?" "Beats me." "They look like ants when you step on their hill." "Shouldn't they stick together?"

Cousin Belle and I exchanged a look. These people clearly knew little about big ships and maybe even less about the deadly attacks that had been happening along our coast for the past five months. They didn't seem to know that just one torpedo could crack a thousand-foot-long freighter in half and sink it in ten minutes flat. Or that some of the Nazi crews were such Hitler lovers they'd surface and strafe a lifeboat. Didn't seem to know that since January hundreds of merchant sailors had already had a ship blown up from under them by Hitler's submariners, or that many of them had perished in waters raging with oil fires, or that those who had survived were so brave, so dedicated, that they signed up to go out to sea again. I wondered how many of the sailors out there on the bay in front of us, fighting the fire or having to abandon ship, had already endured a sinking.

"They're zigzagging," Cousin Belle spoke loudly, so the dopes surrounding us would hear her plain as day. "It's an evasion tactic. Tacking wide and sharply, to make it harder for a U-boat to aim its torpedoes at them. Moving targets, harder to hit."

"U-boats, you say? *Humph.* I figured all that 'loose lips sink ships' stuff was hooey, Roosevelt scamming us to buy his war bonds." A jowly, sun-tanned middle-age man, his belly hanging over his swim trunks, doddered over to us. He sucked on his cigar, eyeing Cousin Belle, clearly perplexed by her turn-of-the-century swim attire and trying to assess her wherewithal, given her appearance.

"Yes, U-boats." Cousin Belle returned his stare. "Zigzagging is a tanker's only defense. Unless a destroyer is right beside a ship. And even then . . ." She shook her head. "Think of a Nazi U-boat as being like an expert sniper hiding underneath miles of water."

At that very moment the sand under my feet shuddered again. *KA-BOOM!*

Way out at the capes, another enormous geyser of water shot heavenward. Then a massive flare of blood-red fire sliced up into the blue skyline, followed by oil-black clouds that obliterated everything. Another shot. Another hit. Another ship swallowed in suffocating, scorching fumes.

I flinched. The crowd gasped. Then we all went dead silent, afraid.

Oh, Butler.

Within a few minutes, I could hear a muffled, spaced out *THUMP-boom*—like distant thunder. One—two—three—four—five. *THUMP-boom.*

"What the hell is that?" the cigar-sucking man fairly shouted.

I'd heard that sound before, when fishing far out around the oyster reefs. Depth charges. Clearly the navy thought there was at least one U-boat lurking in the deep, firing torpedoes at this easy line-up of victims. Until a submarine surfaced, our navy's only way to attack it was to throw a trashcan-size barrel packed with dynamite into the sea, hoping the aftershock waves of its explosion would reach a submerged U-boat and shake it violently enough to damage it.

I squinted to see across the waves better. I could see little balls catapulting off the back end of the destroyer. *THUMP—boom.*

The destroyer was lobbing a real barrage. I kept count, hoping . . . hoping for a hit . . . feeling a little sick for hoping so hard that a crew of Germans were about to meet their doom . . . but sicker at the thought of another American ship, of some other girl's big brother being blown up.

Six—seven—eight. *THUMP-boom.*

The sand shifted and rocked under my feet again. *KA-BOOM.* The hotel rattled in echo. Smoke billowed off the back end of the destroyer.

"Damn it to hell," Cousin Belle muttered.

Had the destroyer been hit? Or had a depth charge exploded too soon before it made the water? Oh my God. What would save those ships now, the men surrounded by those burning waves?

"Miss Archer! There you are."

Cousin Belle turned. Walter was hurrying across the sand. "Come inside, Miss Archer. The folks at Fort Monroe want us to clear the beach." He picked up her big bag of books for her and lowered his voice, "Just in case."

"In case . . . what?" I murmured. Fury billowed up in me. "In case Nazis are going to torpedo boatloads of boys—in broad daylight while a bunch of beachgoers watch and do nothing?" I waved my arms at the men standing around me.

Cousin Belle caught my arm. "Hush, child," she said gently. "This isn't Walter's fault—he's not launching torpedoes and he's not gawking, all gobsmacked. We don't want to spark a panic among these people for him to have to deal with, do we? And the navy is responding. With what it has."

I blinked back tears—of anger, of sorrow, of fear, of frustration.

She squeezed my arm. "Get your things now, honey."

I picked up my shoes and novel. I turned toward the hotel, after taking one more searing look. As if the image of that hellfire wasn't already forever branded into my soul.

Soldiers from the fort were starting to move through the crowd. "Inside, folks. Inside, please."

Walter smiled reassuringly at me as we reached the veranda. "They want everyone off the beach so they don't have to waste men protecting you, miss. That way they can focus on hunting down the U-boat and sending out fireboats. Looking for survivors who jumped and might not have made it to a lifeboat."

Survivors. In the water.

I turned to Cousin Belle and tugged on her sleeve, frantic with an idea. "I need to get home. Right away. Please."

They might have laughed at me at Mr. Cooper's

docks, the idea of my joining the Coastal Pickets. But there was nothing to stop me from taking my family's boat out into the waters to help find survivors—to do what no one had been able to do for Butler.

CHAPTER 20

It was unfair of me to not trust her, but I wasn't sure what Cousin Belle would say about my plan. So I stayed silent on the trip home, brooding, unable to wipe the vision of those ships, that inferno, from my mind and heart.

She respected my silence and just drove, still in her ridiculous swimming dress. Seeing how riled up I was, she had taken me straight to her car. I could feel her eyes on me and knew she was glancing over to assess me, swerving even more than she usually did. I kept my own gaze out the window and prayed she wouldn't hit anything along the road.

As she turned into our driveway, I could see Daddy sitting out in front of the barn, on a turned-over pail, whittling, enjoying the makings of a glorious June sunset. He waved at us. We looped around to the front of the house, and there was Mama sitting on the porch, kittens on her lap, D'Artagnan outstretched in the warm sunbeams at her feet.

"Oh my," Cousin Belle breathed. "Ruth is waiting and watching for you, child. That's . . . that's a tremendously good sign."

I almost let go of my plan, feeling my heart leap up at seeing Mama like that, lit up golden in sunshine, just like a daffodil about to bud. Just like Butler had recited that Wordsworth poem the last night we were all together.

Oh, Butler.

Cousin Belle slowed her car to a stop. Mama smiled, gathered the squirming baby cats into her arms, and called to me, "The kittens want to hear something nice about your adventure today," she called.

There was no time for that. I'd already lost twenty-two minutes on the drive home. It would take me at least an hour to chug my way to the bay's mouth at top speed in our deadrise. Maybe ninety minutes. How long could a person float? How long if he were injured?

I opened the car door. And bolted.

"Louisa June!" Cousin Belle called after me.

I raced on.

"Lou?" Out of the corner of my eye I saw Daddy stand.

I made it to our dock.

"Lou!" I felt Daddy running after me. "What are you doing?"

I yanked off the first loop of rope tying the deadrise to our pier. I dashed to the next piling and pulled that tether.

"Lou! Stop!" I could hear Daddy's feet pounding the boards of the dock.

"Louisa June!" Mama. Mama was up and following me?

I didn't care. Couldn't care. I kept focused on the ropes. I yanked on the third and final noose that would set the deadrise free. It snagged. "C'mon," I shouted, pulling.

"Lou!" Daddy grabbed my arm.

I tried to wrench away. Tried to jump on the boat.

"What's the matter with you?" Daddy held fast. "Lou!"

I kept floundering.

Lighter footfalls on the pier's planking. "Louisa June, honey. What's wrong?"

Still I fought to break loose.

Then in my struggle, I heard a slower trot along those boards. "Child!" That old woman had managed to run? "Tell them," she coughed out, winded. "Tell them what you saw."

Cousin Belle's voice stopped me. I quieted. I looked up at her.

She nodded in understanding. "Now this is the kind of adventure Bilbo would have taken. But remember, child, the hobbit had help. Tell your parents."

I hesitated. There was no way Mama could bear it—not the scene I had just witnessed. She'd blanched this morning at the thought of German chocolate cake. She'd passed out seeing my stitches. *Don't tell Mama. Don't upset her.* Butler had protected her from knowing an empty life jacket had drifted up into our cove. How could she handle the image of an exploding ship? She'd know, just as I did. *That was what it had looked like.*

I shook my head at Cousin Belle.

"I'll start then," she said. She took Mama's hand. "Ruth, when we were at the Chamberlin, we saw a convoy of merchant ships coming through the capes into port and—"

"Two of them blew up!" The words just erupted out of me. Cousin Belle was taking too long. "It had to have been torpedoes. From U-boats."

Daddy's face went ashen.

I plucked at his shirt. "Sailors had to abandon ship. They're sure to be some in the water, Daddy. I want . . . please . . . I want to go help." I dared to look Mama's way, assuming she had fainted again.

But she hadn't.

"Mama?" I dared. "Mama, please. There could be . . . there could be . . ."

"A boy like Butler," she murmured.

"Yes."

Mama looked down for a moment, looked heavenward, looked at Cousin Belle, looked back to me, biting her lip. Then she slowly turned toward Daddy and raised her eyes to his. The very first time she had since that awful, awful night. But unlike that soul-wrenching moment of madness, she was dead calm. "You should go," she said.

Daddy sucked in his breath. Tears streaked his face. And suddenly he looked tall again.

"Lou, we'll need some extra lamps and flashlights to search the water," he ordered in his captain's voice. "They're some in the barn. Run get them. I'll gas her up."

I raced and came back, my hands full. I scrambled onto the boat as Daddy turned over the engine, and it roared into life, sounding much stronger after its do-over by the army.

"Wait," Mama called over the motor. "I'm coming with you."

"No way, Ruthie," Daddy shouted back. "It's too—"

"Dangerous?" Mama gestured to me to lend her a hand so she could hop safely into the boat.

I looked to Daddy for permission.

"Russell, you will need to steer," Mama insisted. "Louisa June will need to be on watch. And . . . and . . . if any boy you find is hurt, he'll need someone to tend to him. Maybe if someone could have reached Butler . . . maybe . . ." She paused. I waited for Mama to trail off and disappear into her fog of sadness. But she didn't. She regathered herself. "You need three hands for this voyage."

I couldn't believe it—how collected Mama was.

"Ruthie, no. You don't want to see ships aflame." Daddy clearly had the same doubt I did about Mama being able to hold together, sailing into hell. "Trust me," he added, under his breath.

His words jarred me. Suddenly, I wondered if he would hold together either. If part of the reason Daddy had hidden in the barn all these weeks was because he was shouting out in nightmares, too.

The three of us froze as the engine idled, unsure of one another. Unsure of ourselves.

"Russell," Cousin Belle's voice cut through. "Don't be a fool."

The advice she had given me a few weeks ago flew back at me. *You can't fix your mama. She has to fight her battles herself and to want to do so. Finding that resolve when lost in darkness is the hardest. What you can do to help her is to show that you have faith in her.*

I gave Mama my hand. She clambered in. We cast off. The three of us, hurt souls all, but together.

CHAPTER 21

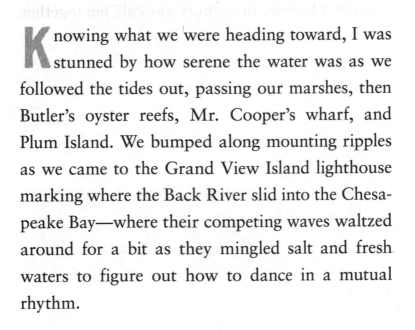

Knowing what we were heading toward, I was stunned by how serene the water was as we followed the tides out, passing our marshes, then Butler's oyster reefs, Mr. Cooper's wharf, and Plum Island. We bumped along mounting ripples as we came to the Grand View Island lighthouse marking where the Back River slid into the Chesapeake Bay—where their competing waves waltzed around for a bit as they mingled salt and fresh waters to figure out how to dance in a mutual rhythm.

Then we were out onto the open bay and its constant chop. But even there, the growing twilight was peaceful, no winds, and the warm air had smoothed out those deeper waters into a tranquil mirror.

Mama and Daddy stayed silent. At the wheel, he was intent on navigating and making good time. Mama sat on the stern's bench. She was gazing up at the rosy sunset skies. I was tucked in next to her, ready to grab her hand when those ships' volcano of flames would appear in the distance.

Looking back over her shoulder toward land, she whispered, "Star light, star bright, first star I see tonight." She pointed to a glowing dot just above the tree line. "Look there, Louisa June. It's Venus."

"I thought the North Star was the first star to come out at night."

"Nope," Daddy answered from the helm. "It's Venus. The planet named for love." He glanced back at Mama and then forward again.

"I wish I may," she nudged me.

"I wish I might," I answered.

In unison, we ended: "Have the wish we wish tonight."

Mama sighed. I knew she was thinking on Butler, his last words to us about how beautiful the stars were out on the water, the reflection of them in the ocean, the communion of sea and sky. Tears glistened on her face. What would I do if she fell apart out here?

"Good God," Daddy groaned. He slowed the engine. Before us the ocean was afire.

Slowly, Mama stood. "Lord, have mercy."

I felt a gut-punch of nausea. The blaze on the one ship looked even bigger, the smoldering squall line of smoke even more evil against the setting sun's pink clouds. I rose and slipped my hand into Mama's. I heard her exhale, "Oh, Butler." I felt her tremble.

That was what it had looked like.

Coming toward us, backlit by hell, was a flotilla of local fishing boats.

"It's Ed Cooper." Daddy cupped his hands

around his mouth to shout, "Coop! Hey Coop!"

Mr. Cooper waved and turned his boat to approach us. His dog, Captain, sat on the bow like one of those mermaids on an old whaling ship, and the elder Mr. Cooper stooped beside it. "Captain Brookes! Sir! I wish to speak with you!" His reedy voice floated across the water, and I could hear Mr. Cooper shush him. "Not now, Pop."

Cutting our engine, Dad waited for Mr. Cooper to pull alongside, while the other boats continued on, heading home to land. When we bobbed twenty yards apart, but within easy shouting, Daddy called, "What's it look like out there?"

"Two tankers hit bad. One half sunk, bow down, burning. Blocking the channel out to sea. One hundred thousand barrels of crude leaking. Oil fires everywhere." Mr. Cooper thumbed back over his shoulder toward the blaze. "They've got fireboats trying to kill the flames in the hull. We went out to see if they needed help fishing crew out of the water."

"Same here," Daddy shouted. "Everyone accounted for?"

"Yes, siree! Ain't that a miracle? All saved, except one poor soul, who must have died in the explosion. The ships were hit so close in to Virginia Beach the Twenty-Fourth Street coast guard station was able to get most of them. Can you believe them Nazis were sharking around in Thimble Shoals? Looks like they knew exactly where to lie in wait in the shallows and when to make their ambush. Like someone drew them a chart map. Or gave them a shipping schedule. Damnedest thing."

We all fell silent contemplating what that could mean. After a tick, Daddy asked, "Why you heading back?"

"Almost out of gas."

"Think they still need help?"

"What's left is up to the big boys now," Mr. Cooper answered. "The fire is out in the second tanker. But she's listing bad, drifting seaward, so she can't do nothing for herself. Three tugs are out there trying to pull her into Lynnhaven Roads to salvage her diesel cargo. But their towlines keep snapping."

I saw Daddy straighten, his jaw grind, at the mention of tugboats.

"I 'spect they're going to be at it all night," Mr. Cooper continued. "Poor bastards. That tanker's a sitting duck the way she is. She and all those tug crews. The *Bainbridge* was out earlier, dropping depth charges to try to nail those Nazi devils, but looks like she got hit, too. Mangled her propellers. She's limped back to port. So all they've got is a coast guard cutter circling the stranded tanker to protect her from being torpedoed again."

Daddy scowled. His hands started trembling. I'd never seen that before. "What tugs?" he asked. "Are they attaching the cables right?"

At that, the elder Cooper just couldn't contain himself anymore. "Precisely my point," he barked at his son. Then he turned to Daddy. "We need captains and seaman that know what they're doing to be out there, what with the Nazis on the hunt. When you take your next run, Captain Brookes, sign me up. I'm ready."

"Pop, for—" Mr. Cooper broke off abruptly. He obviously was about to say a pretty foul word and had just spotted Mama. He tugged on the brim of his cap. "Ruth, ma'am, good to see you." He nodded at me. "Louisa." Then he made a face at his father, trying to shut him up.

But the elder Mr. Cooper was determined. "When are you going out next, Captain?"

"I'm not going back out on a tug." Daddy's voice was quiet, seemingly matter-of-fact, but I could see his face, and it was anything but unemotional.

"What?" Mr. Cooper was stunned. "Why the hell not?" he blurted.

Daddy grimaced and abruptly turned our deadrise's engine back on. He shouted over its rumble, "Be seeing you, Coop," as he shoved the throttle forward to propel us away.

"But, Captain!" the old man cried. "They need you!"

Daddy's face clouded into a storm. He shifted into high gear. Mama fell back onto the bench at the lurch and bounce-bounce-bounce as our deadrise rushed, skipping up and over waves. Spray slapped up over the bow, dousing us in stinging salt water. I staggered forward. "Daddy, slow down!"

He spotted another pack of fishermen heading back to their wharves. Daddy sped up even more. To avoid their asking him questions, too. Questions, I realized, for the first time, skewered him like harpoons. Questions he couldn't bear to answer. He swerved, hard, away. I fell into the cabin roof when he did.

"I'm not tugging again," Daddy muttered. "I don't want another crew." He shook and shook and shook his head, talking to himself. "No more boys that I might get blown up."

He tacked again. I fell to the deck. This time I cried out in pain.

Daddy kept going.

"Russell! Stop it!" Mama had somehow made it to his side, fighting the pitch and roll of his zigzag. "Stop it! Do you want to kill another of our children?"

Daddy covered his ears, letting go of the wheel. The boat shimmied and skewed, unguided, wild.

This could kill all of us.

I got onto my knees and lunged at the wheel. I pulled back on the throttle. We bucked, then slowed, the boat shuddering down to a float.

Daddy was sobbing. "I couldn't find him. I couldn't find him. I called and called, Ruthie. He just . . . he didn't answer. I called . . . nothing . . . anywhere. I think . . . I think we lost him when the engine room exploded. That's when I got thrown into the sea. I think that . . . If I just hadn't . . . hadn't . . . the navy thinks . . ."

I held my breath. *No, no, no. Don't say it.*

Daddy was choking on his sobs now, inaudible, doubled over. Then he managed to gasp out, "He just never answered."

I will love my daddy for all eternity that he didn't tell Mama that the navy believed his phone call home that night to reassure her had been the lure that brought on Butler's killers.

I looked up at Mama. She was shaking. Her face was streaked with bay water and tears and grief. But she was looking right at Daddy. She was with us. She knelt. She gathered him into her arms.

And I saw Daddy breathe again.

KA-BOOM!

The earth rocked.

KA-BOOM!

We turned and looked, aghast, toward the horizon. Out beyond the burning tanker was a new fireball. But this explosion was like a thousand fireworks gone crazy. From the waterline shot up spears of flames carrying dark masses that arched and plummeted into the waves, making enormous geysers of spray, and then burst into smaller fires.

Still holding one another, Mama and Daddy stood. "That ship has ruptured and exploded," he said grimly. "No chance to launch lifeboats. Just like . . ." He trailed off.

That was what it had looked like.

Mama bit her lip.

"Life jackets?" I managed to croak.

"If they were smart, they had them on already." He pulled away from Mama, holding her at arms' length. "You okay, Ruthie?"

She nodded and drew in a big breath. "Let's go."

"You sure?"

"Yes," she answered. "I trust you."

I felt myself rejoice at her words.

❧

Night fell quickly as we made our way down the bay toward its burning mouth. The moon rose big, full, and low. It spilled a ribbon of pearly silver along the waters to us, like a carpet from heaven, just like Butler had described. It was so bizarre that the universe went on being luminous and gorgeous even as we humans set fire to it.

We were still a few miles from the flames and smoke when we started bumping up into debris. Smoldering planks. A half-submerged chair. Clouds of canvas, wafting outstretched, deadly nets to anything that might drift into them. Daddy slowed to a crawl, fearing we might get caught in the material's webbing. I leaned over our boat's edge, watching for other unseen snags that might scuttle us. Looking for a periscope. Searching for a crewmember to save.

I started to tremble a bit myself. How would

I feel if I saw a lifeless body? What should I do? *Don't tell Mama.* I glanced back at her. Mama's face was lit in an eerie reddish light from the purgatory we were approaching. But so far she was holding on.

"Dammit," Daddy cursed. "Our gas is low. We can only stay out here another ten minutes."

"But, Daddy," I protested. I knew he was right. I knew if we ran out of gas here, we could be pushed out to sea on the tides. But the blistering need to do something to help our boys, something to stop the Nazis, made me burst into tears. "But, Daddy," I whimpered.

"Shh, listen." Mama held up her hand up to her ear.

I began to hear the splutter of faster boats ahead. Had to be coast guard search-and-rescue. I cocked my head and closed my eyes to make my ears keener. I made out: "Over here!" "Hang on, sir. We've got you."

Daddy nodded at me. "The cavalry's here."

He turned the boat for home.

I'm ashamed to share how disappointed I was.

It wasn't natural to want to find a floating body, hopefully a live one, of course. But still. I sank onto the deck and leaned my chin on the boat's ledge, trying to dredge up normalcy from deep inside me, left over from the before of all this, like Butler had walked along its planking, tonging oysters.

Our deadrise splashed along the now-dark waters, for about ten minutes, before I realized Mama was talking to herself. I looked back at her and could tell she was slipping into that terrible world of fog. Only then did I realize it must have felt important to her as well to find a boy to save. As some sort of counterbalance. As if we could pull up Butler out of the sea and bring him back to us.

"Peaceful and beautiful," she murmured. "The heavens and clouds reflected." She looked up at the sky, now abloom with constellations. She had that bone-chilling soothsayer expression about her. "The Milky Way so brilliant." She trailed her hand in the water. "Stars in the waves."

She lowered her gaze to the bay. "Stars in the waves."

I knew what she was quoting: Butler's last words to her. I felt fear chill me at the tone of her voice.

"Stars in the waves. Stars in the waves."

"Mama?" I stood.

"Ruthie?" Daddy had turned from the wheel.

She pointed. "Stars in the waves. Stars in the waves!"

And before we could reach her, Mama plunged into the deep.

"Mama!" I screamed. I stepped onto the boat's ledge, but Daddy grabbed me.

He shoved a flashlight into my hand. "Shine that on her," he commanded and revved the boat.

"Mama!" I cried again, swinging my tiny searchlight. "MAAA-MA!" *Don't do this to me, Mama. Don't do this.* I finally caught a splash in the beam and managed to home in on her. She was swimming, hard, fighting the tide, floundering. "MAMA! STOP!"

"Don't lose her, Lou," Daddy told me, turning the boat toward her. Then he shouted, a horrible catch in his voice, "RUTHIE, PLEASE!"

"Oh my God!" I sucked in my breath. "Daddy! Look! There's something out there. She's swimming toward something."

Half submerged, a little light flickering on his life jacket like a twinkling star, was a boy.

THE
ALL
OF IT

CHAPTER 22

"We see him, Ruthie!" Daddy called over the engine. "We're coming! Hang on." His shout to Mama was calm, but when he turned to me it shook. "Keep that light on her, Lou. Right on her, you hear? We get your mama first, the boy next."

"Yes, sir," I murmured, clutching the flashlight with both hands to try to keep it steady against my trembling. In its beam we could see Mama thrashing, pushed back by the current, struggling to battle through it. *Hang on, Mama. Hang on.*

She was almost to the boy, who bobbed and swirled in the swells, like an autumn leaf fallen into a creek. My flashlight beam caught him clearly now too. He was unconscious, his head lolling, held above inky water only by his life jacket. Was he alive?

We were almost to Mama, just a few more yards. Almost. . .

Suddenly, I didn't see Mama at all. "MAMA!" I cried.

"RUTHIE!" Daddy echoed. "RUTHIE!"

Nothing.

"MAMA!"

Daddy cut the engine, afraid the boat might overrun her. "RUTHIE!" He lunged to the boat's edge, leaning over, searching the dark waters beneath us. "RUTHIE!"

No sound but our shouts and the waves slapping the deadrise. The tide was pushing the boy closer now, the little beacon on his jacket no longer twinkling, burned out, his arms spread wide, limp like a broken bird. Like a terrifying omen.

"MAMA!" I swept the flashlight beam back and forth frantically. "MA-MAAA!"

Nothing.

Suddenly, Butler's voice, true and sweet, in a snippet of a recitation, called to me:

> No stain
> Can come upon the visage of the moon
> When it has looked in glory from a cloud.

Butler. The moon. Stars in the waves. I turned my eyes to a river of shimmering light cast by the moon along the otherwise shadowy waters that the boy was drifting toward.

In those glittering waves, a hand rose up. I saw it—a pale, fragile hand. It grabbed the edge of the boy's life jacket. And Mama surfaced, haloed in silvery light, gagging, coughing, holding tight to the boy.

"There she is, Daddy!" I pointed. "There!"

"Take the wheel. Keep the boat steady," Daddy commanded. He dove into the deep. Within a few urgent strokes, he reached Mama and grabbed her arm. Daddy tugged hard, towing her and the dead-weight boy to me. He pushed Mama up and in first. Then the two of us hauled while Daddy shoved. The boy slid over our deadrise's edge and onto its deck, bleeding water.

His face was bloody. His hands were burned, his jacket singed. But the boy was breathing. He was alive.

"Quick, Louisa," Mama said through chattering teeth, "help me wrap him in those blankets I brought."

We cocooned the boy quickly as Daddy scrambled over the boat's lip, bringing another gush of water with him. He crawled to Mama and crushed her in his arms. "Don't ever leave me like that again, Ruthie. Please," he murmured. "That . . . that was way too risky. Promise me."

She smiled and nodded and touched his face. Then she motioned for me. I fell into their arms, the three of us shuddering, trying to ease down together.

"I'm sorry if I frightened you, June-Bug," Mama whispered into my hair.

Fleetingly, I thought of the hundreds of times that Mama had frightened me—badly—not knowing if she would ever come back to us out of the thick, seething mists of her mind. This time had been different. "I . . . I thought you were very brave, Mama."

She pulled back a little to look into my face. "Really?" Mama squeezed me and murmured, "I just followed your lead, sugar. Your infuriating, wonderfully headstrong lead." Then she looked to Daddy. "We better get this boy help quickly. Can we make it to Norfolk?"

"Not enough gas. We'll get him home first. Your crazy cousin will likely still be there. She helped nurse the wounded, didn't she?—God save them."

"Yes, Daddy, she did."

Daddy startled a little at my protectiveness of Cousin Belle and then grinned at me. "Well then, it's a good thing the old bird is there. If nothing else, she can get us to the hospital in that fancy, juiced-up car of hers." He stood. "Lou, go below and get your mama my jacket."

Once Mama was cloaked and no longer shivering, Daddy went back to the helm.

She settled in by the boy, cradling his head on her lap. As Daddy turned over the engine, and it gave a little pop and jolt, the boy stirred. He woke.

He gazed up at Mama and spoke in accent I barely understood. "Mum," he murmured, delirious, "I'm so glad to see you, Mum." Then he closed his eyes, a peaceful smile on his face.

"Well, I'll be," said Daddy. "There's a cockney for you, Lou."

❧

Cousin Belle was indeed on our pier, pacing, when we reached it. She'd already brought out bandages and ointments from the barn and our medicine cabinet, anticipating, hoping, believing that we'd bring back a soul in need of tending. Even Daddy couldn't criticize how efficiently she checked the boy for broken bones, splinted his ankle, wrapped his burns, and helped us get him laid out flat and safe in the enormous back seat of her Ford coupe.

Before she got in to drive, she took Mama's hand and peered at her long and hard, through those thick cat glasses of hers. She liked what she saw in Mama's face. "Butler would be proud of you, Ruth. I know I am."

Mama bit her lip. Even in the gloom of midnight I could see tears well up in her eyes.

I caught my breath with worry at how Mama might react to the mention of Butler.

But she didn't retreat. She just hugged Cousin Belle. And the old lady rocked her.

Finally, Cousin Belle pulled away, cleared her throat, and issued instructions. "Child, you ride with me in case this boy wakes as we drive him. Ruth, go inside, take a hot bath, and put on some dry clothes right away to ward off the chills. Russell, make sure she does it. Then call the naval hospital to tell them we're coming and who we're bringing." She paused and added with a wry smile, "I do believe you know how to use that telephone now?"

Daddy actually chuckled. "Yes, ma'am," he said, saluting her.

As we drove away, Cousin Belle took my hand. "Now that, child. That is what I would call an adventure."

❧

The boy stayed unconscious as we drove those thirty-plus minutes to the hospital, which Cousin Belle told me was probably the best thing for him, so he wouldn't be frightened. When I asked her how she knew that, she allowed as how she had driven an ambulance during the war once or twice. Of course she had, I thought.

So I didn't find out until later—when Mama and I visited the boy on the ward—who he was exactly. Turns out he was a nineteen-year-old signalman on a *British* trawler. One of a small squadron of big ocean-going fishing vessels that England had refitted with machine guns and depth charges and sent over to help us survive the onslaught of Hitler's U-boats until we could build enough of our own ships to protect ourselves.

His name is Bertie. He is indeed from London. Before he was shipped home to recuperate, he told me what it was like to live near Big Ben and the Tower of London, about flying kites in Hyde Park just like the Banks children did in *Mary Poppins*. He also talked about his worries—about the bombs the Luftwaffe was dropping on his city, about his family's safety. I hated saying goodbye to him and prayed that the ship carrying Bertie back to England would be in a convoy Will was leading. My big brother would watch out for him. I also superstitiously thought Bertie was good luck since he'd been one of the blessed ones aboard his trawler. Only a dozen of his crew survived that horrifying night. Eighteen others died when their trawler hit a mine and that explosion then detonated the ship's arsenal, shattering the ship instantly.

That's right, a mine. Not a torpedo. Turns out a U-boat had managed to get pretty deep into the Chesapeake Bay undetected, using Norfolk landmarks illuminated on shore as a guide, and left behind a string of death in the shipping channel. Then the Nazis slipped back out to sea with no one ever knowing they had been there.

A fourth ship—a freighter—would explode and go down before the navy was able to sweep the waters with metal detectors and implode all the mines the U-boat had left.

Virginia finally started dousing its lights at night.

Mama still has the melancholy. But she tries hard to combat the storm-surge purple-black. She looks for the right sprinkle of sunshine to help dispel the fogs. It isn't easy. She doesn't always succeed. But she's stronger than I thought—Cousin Belle was right about that. Fishing that boy out of burning waves helped make her want to fight again. And for some reason, those kittens troop right along behind her, which is always good for a little smile when she needs it.

Daddy has refound purpose. He is taking out tugs again, to keep the country supplied, to fight the Nazis. And Mr. Cooper the elder crews for him. Daddy says he's a hell of a radioman.

I'm helping Emmett memorize all those plane silhouettes so he can join the Ground Observers Corps. The differences in aircraft are subtle—being aerodynamic requires a basic structure, after all. Emmett isn't exactly the studious sort, but he sure is knuckling down to learn them.

I've promised to search the skies with him twice a week, and the navy has outfitted our deadrise with a secure radio, so I can report anything I might spot when I'm out among the oyster beds. You can bet the farm I will be looking and watching. I'm also volunteering at the hospital, reading to survivors of U-boat attacks, because they're in need of "somethings nice" to listen to as they recuperate. Cousin Belle says that when we take the fight to Hitler, landing our troops in North Africa sometime later this year, there'll be hurt GIs sent home in need of a good read, too. I figure spending time around doctors and nurses will also help me know if I have an appetite for medicine and finding cures for troubles like Mama's. Cousin Belle goes with me. And when Katie can take the time, we pick her up from the shipyard for lunch and laugh over her stories about the shipyard.

e∼ɔ

We are not the same as we were before, of course. How could we be? Grief walks with us. And there are days I can hardly breathe, thinking about Butler and missing him. But I do what he told me, when trouble blows up, I steer my little boat straight in and hold tight to the rudder. I'm studying hard to deserve his legacy that Cousin Belle set up for me at the bank.

Mama gave me that pearl Butler had shucked out of a gray, crinkly oyster shell, covered with barnacles, mud worms, and sea squirts. He always did know how to find the beautiful, the mystical—like stars in the waves. I'm hoping I can, too.

AUTHOR'S NOTE

As always, I need to thank the wondrous Katherine Tegen for her narrative vision, her refined edits, and her faith in me—especially with this novel that features a more intimate and idiosyncratic first-person voice than I usually use for historical novels. And, of course, my son and daughter, Peter and Megan, a professional writer and theater artist, who so helped me find my course on this journey. They shared their truly brilliant thoughts on themes, characters, and plot choices while encouraging mine when I doubted myself, and offered deft, revelatory notes, wrapped without fail in love and support.

Louisa June's story is about many things: World War II on our home front, sudden loss, grief, family, and emotional health. While she and her family are fictitious, the wartime events that anchor this novel are fact.

Just weeks after Japan's devastating surprise attack on Pearl Harbor, a small fleet of Hitler's U-boat submarines *(Unterseeboot)*, arrived on our East Coast and began hunting down civilian merchant ships. Their goal: to seed fear along our shores, slow our ability to ramp up our own defenses, and sever American supply lines to England. If Britain was starved of fuel, food, and military supplies, it would likely fall—also denying the United States a launching pad for any invasion of Nazi-occupied Europe.

Hitler's U-boats struck at night. Their crews easily spotted the silhouettes of American vessels backlit by the illuminated skylines of East Coast cities, and then sank them, without warning, often with just one torpedo and within fifteen minutes of the hit. Not

Poster created for the Office of Emergency Management by Glenn Grohe, 1942, to warn against "careless talk" that could be picked up by radio-operators on Nazi U-boats trolling the East Coast. (courtesy National Archives)

anticipating attacks on our own territory, the United States was woefully ill prepared to protect ships and crew or to fight back—short on spotter planes, modern warships, antisubmarine weaponry, and training. Half the US Navy warships were in the Pacific, and fourteen of those had been severely damaged during Pearl Harbor. Compounding the problem was the fact that two years earlier, to help shore up Britain, we'd sent them fifty World War I–era destroyers in exchange for land leases in Newfoundland, Bermuda, and the British West Indies. All we had left were a dozen old destroyers and small coast guard cutters to patrol 28,000 miles of shoreline from Florida to Maine. As a result, for many months, our merchant ships traveled our coastal water shipping lanes mostly unescorted, essentially sitting ducks.

From January to July 1942—before mandated nightly blackouts, before our radar and sonar were fully effective, before observation towers could be built, before aircrew and the coast guard were well trained in locating and combating U-boats hidden in the ocean—a mere five U-boats managed to sink 397 freighters and tankers off our coast. A million tons of cargo destroyed, dozens of Americans lost each night, those who survived their ship's blast often drifting on the open seas for days before being rescued.

In the month of March alone, Hitler's U-boats sank thirty-three tankers, freighters, and cargo ships a week, one every eight hours, most within sight of land. Nazis crews called it "the Happy Time."

Hitler's primary targets were New York and the opening of the Chesapeake Bay in southern Virginia, at Norfolk-Hampton Roads. Not only was that area an enormous commercial shipping center, it was home to half a dozen military bases as well as shipyards and factories quickly converted to producing wartime armaments. Residents from Tidewater Virginia to North Carolina's Outer Banks dealt constantly with oil slicks, debris, and sometimes even broken bodies washing up in their inlets and beaches. Some grimly joked they could read at night by the glow of ships burning a few miles out to sea.

It wasn't until April that American sailors spotted and successfully battled a U-boat. The USS *Jesse Roper*, a patrolling World War I–vintage destroyer, unleashed a barrage of depth charges to sink U-85 near Cape

Hatteras, NC. The navy buried the crew with full honors in Hampton National Cemetery as I describe Louisa June and Katie witnessing in chapter 13. (The *Jesse Roper* was also the ship that saved the real-life "lifeboat baby" Louisa June reads about in chapter 8.)

Poster created by Seymour Goff coined what became one of the most famous warnings of the war, 1942. (courtesy National Archives)

Some German captains would throw water or provisions to survivors before submerging and disappearing into the dark waters to continue their hunt. One of the most poignant examples of such mercy is the *Laconia* incident, when U-156 sank a British ocean liner it suspected of transporting troops and supplies, only to discover the vessel was carrying hundreds of civilian passengers as well. Captain Werner Hartenstein rescued them, taking many on board and tethering to his U-boat several lifeboats crammed with survivors. Staying on the surface while negotiating with the Allies to come take its civilians exposed his own sub and crew to attack. Within hours, U-156 was indeed bombarded by an American bomber. (If you're interested, there is a marvelous two-part BBC TV movie, *The Sinking of the Laconia*.)

Other U-boat captains were ruthless. Butler's death in this story was inspired by a particularly brutal attack by U-754 on a hundred-and-forty-foot tugboat, the *Menominee*, on March 31, 1942. U-754 blasted the tugboat's cabin and sank the three barges of coal and lumber the *Menominee* was towing—achieving the Nazis' mission to eliminate fuel and supplies. But Captain Johannes Oestermann ordered his crew to finish off the *Menominee*, even though the small boat's radio had been destroyed in their initial barrage, meaning there was no danger of the tug alerting American authorities about the submarine's presence. U-754 chased down the tugboat and shelled it with its deck guns, setting it ablaze. The *Menominee* exploded seconds later. Only a handful of its crewmembers reached a life raft and lattice float. And only three of them survived the night until they were spotted the next morning by a tanker on its way to New York.

The crew of the *Northern Sun* knew they risked being torpedoed by the U-boat, which could be lingering near the wreckage, submerged and invisible, watching for a new target. But it stopped anyway. A lifeboat was lowered. When its engine gave out, the sailors manning it knew every passing moment was critical to the *Menominee* survivors in the frigid water, and they rowed so hard they snapped an oar. They found a seventeen-year-old boy clinging to the floatation's wooden latticework so desperately, his rescuers had to pry his fingers loose. Heartbreakingly, after the crew battled to "to get the water out of him," the teenager died in the tanker's sickbay from a broken neck and severed spinal cord. It had been his very first voyage.

There were two sets of fathers and sons on the *Menominee*. The captain and his son, an able seaman; and the cook and his son, a messman. Both sons were twenty-two years old. Neither survived.

During World War II, the US government ordered the construction of 2,751 Liberty cargo ships, like the ones Katie helps weld together at the Newport

News Shipbuilding and Dry Docks Company. Eighteen of those Liberty Boats were named after African Americans—including one for the young messman who perished on the *Menominee*, George A. Lawson. Another was for William Cox, a forty-four-year-old firefighter on a coal-carrying steamer, the *Atwater*, which was ambushed by a different U-boat, two days later and in virtually the same waters as the *Menominee*, just off Virginia's Eastern Shore at Chincoteague Inlet. All but three of its twenty-five crewmembers perished, most machine-gunned by the Nazis while scrambling to launch lifeboats.

Amazingly, merchant mariners remained undeterred by such horror stories. They re-upped even after having a ship torpedoed out from under them. By the end of the war, one out of eight had experienced his ship going down. Yet retirees like the elder Mr. Cooper reenlisted in droves, so the ages of these civilian sailors during World War II stretched from sixteen to seventy-eight. Ten percent were Black. (Many African American workers also won their first mainstream industrial jobs, building Liberty ships in newly

integrated assembly
lines.) Besides being
our first racially inte-
grated service, the
American Merchant
Marine suffered the
highest casualty rate
of any service during
World War II, losing
9,521 of its sailors.

Two African American welders close-up
(courtesy National Archives)

O ther civilian mariners—commercial fishers and
private yacht owners—also showed extraordinary grit and determination to help the war effort,
joining what was officially called the Coastal Picket
Force or Corsair Fleet but fondly nicknamed the Hoo-
ligan Navy. Trawlers and fishing boats whose captains
were deemed trustworthy in terms of their discretion
were outfitted with secure radios to report anything
suspicious to the Naval Operating Base in Norfolk. In

terms of actually patrolling the coastline, large sailing yachts capable of cruising a hundred and fifty miles offshore—in good and rough weather—were preferred. Under sail, they ran silently, without motors that submerged U-boats could hear from below. These seventy-foot-plus schooners were repainted battleship gray, armed with a single .30-caliber World War I machine gun, a few service rifles, and, if large enough, four depth charges. Their real mission, though, was to spot, track, and radio for backup. Many proved exceedingly important in search-and-rescue as well, using boat hooks and flashlights to locate and pull drowning, burned merchant sailors from the ocean.

In Virginia, picket boats operated out of Little Creek near the mouth of the Chesapeake Bay. The owners served as captain and took on volunteer crews of college students, boy scouts, even former bootleggers and rumrunners. In the rush to get them out to sea as quickly as possible in 1942, the crews received next to no training, the assumption being they were already experienced, expert sailors. Boats were sent on five-day patrols of designated fifteen-square nautical miles,

Many women, like Louisa June's sister, helped build Liberty Boats as welders. These women worked at Shipbuilding Corp, Pascagoula, MS.(courtesy National Archives)

even in winter when the crew fought to keep their rigging from icing over. Some, to maintain radio silence, brought along carrier pigeons trained to fly back to Virginia Beach's Fort Story.

The dangers for them were very real. One sailboat reported grazing a submerged mine as it raced through the bay's opening to the safety of port to escape a quickly gathering hurricane. Another spotted a U-boat running on the surface to recharge its batteries. The Nazi sub dove and then resurfaced directly underneath the small schooner, like a vengeful Moby Dick, lifting the Americans out of the water and scraping the sailboat's bottom as it cruised away. On the other hand, one German U-boat captain in concern for a different sailboat crew, used "excellent Americanese" to shout at them: "Get the hell out of here, you guys! Do you want to get hurt? Scram!"

On shore, Americans walked beaches at dawn, looking for footprints and indications of German saboteurs being landed, or joined Confidential Observation Corps like the Ground Observers of the Aircraft Warning Service—as does Louisa June's friend, Emmett. (If you're interested in learning more about teenage plane watchers, you might enjoy *Across a War-Tossed Sea,* my home front companion novel to *Under a War-Torn Sky.* In it, characters also encounter German POWs and the top-secret, decoy airfield of plywood planes built just outside Richmond, meant to lure the Luftwaffe away from the state's capital city if a Nazi invasion came.)

Virginians felt particularly vulnerable to attack after those four ships entering the Chesapeake Bay exploded in plain sight of Virginia Beach sunbathers in June 1942, as described in the final chapters of this novel. Their paranoia escalated when locals realized that if a Nazi sub had managed to leave a string of lethal magnetic mines in the bay—totally undetected—the crew either had maps to the channel to avoid running aground in shallows or they had followed an unsuspecting American ship in and out. Turns out U-701 had followed a patrolling American trawler as well as navigating by the Cape Henry and Cape Charles lighthouses that still sent their beams out along the Atlantic, welcoming voyagers to the Chesapeake.

With Newport News shipyards and docks in overdrive to build and launch ships, the war was rarely far from residents' minds. That was particularly true for anyone living near Plum Island, where residents heard the boom of bombs exploding as aircrews from Langley ran practice dives over its marshes. Now a wildlife preserve, some of the island has remained closed to the public ever since the war because of the worry of unexploded World War II ordinances remaining half-buried in its sands and mud.

Cousin Belle has been one of my all-time favorite characters to write. She's inspired in part by an ancient lady I loved and called my surrogate grandmother, an audacious intellect who was an attorney with the State Department in the 1930s and '40s. Cousin Belle refers to two women we should all know about. First, Congresswoman Edith Rogers, a Gray Lady during World War I, who then served in the US House for thirty-five years, where she opposed child labor, advocated for equal pay for equal work and a forty-eight-hour workweek for women. In 1939, she co-sponsored a bill to allow twenty thousand German Jewish children under the age of fourteen to settle in the United States, which tragically was not passed by Congress. Having been a volunteer overseas herself, Rogers became a champion for veterans in general and servicewomen especially. Rogers introduced legislation that created the Woman's Army Auxiliary Corps (WAAC) and co-sponsored the GI Bill that sent so many veterans to college after the war. She served in Congress, wearing a trademark orchid or gardenia on her shoulder, until she died at age seventy-nine in 1960.

Cousin Belle also speaks about Lucile Atcherson Curtis, our first female diplomat. A Smith College grad and suffragette, Curtis volunteered in France in 1917, winning the *Medaille de la Reconnaissance Francaise*. In 1920, she took the diplomatic service exam to apply for what would become the US Foreign Service. Despite achieving the third-highest score of that year and being nominated by President Harding, the Senate refused to approve her appointment, saying it was not appropriate for a young single woman to travel overseas alone as a representative of the United States. After much pressure from women's groups, she was sent to Berne, Switzerland, as the third secretary of our delegation.

e‚o

Finally, a word about Mama's "melancholy." Although Cousin Belle's suggestions are practical, proactive actions that psychotherapists recommend today, in 1942, there were no truly viable treatments for profound depression or anxiety disorders. A daughter like Louisa June had few places to turn for help for her mother. At that point there was little comprehension that mental health issues were medical conditions, stemming from physical, biochemical imbalances and genetic vulnerabilities—which life events could ignite or exacerbate—as surely as things like diabetes or heart disease. So people like Mama who battled depression or anxiety were subject to misunderstanding and unkind judgments from their community. If they were hospitalized, they often had to endure well intended but horribly flawed treatments such as being put into steam cabinets from the neck down or submerged in cold-water wraps to "calm their nerves."

That was then.

Today, depression and anxiety are better understood and effectively treated with medicines and talk therapy. According to the National Alliance on Mental Health, one in five adults experiences emotional health issues or mood disorders, and in 75 percent of cases the symptoms began by age twenty-four. The good news is that a regimen of medication and talk therapy will bring significant relief within eight weeks in 60 percent of people. And yet, the average delay between onset and treatment is eleven years—a tragic delay. The harm and heartbreak of sufferers not seeking help or being denied it by insurance companies can spill over onto family and children as well, sometimes with deep, detrimental impact.

You are not alone—if you feel someone you love is suffering these conditions ask adults you know and trust (teachers, neighbors, scout leaders, coaches, ministers, extended family) or medical experts (like your family doctor) for help. You can also call these anonymous hotlines for advice: 800-273-TALK and the National Alliance on Mental Illness at 800-950-NAMI. For help geared specifically to teens, see the JED Foundation: www.jedfoundation.org/mental-health-resource-center/.